THE INVISIBILITY CLOAK

GE FEI is the pen name of Liu Yong, who was born in Jiangsu Province in 1964. He graduated with a degree in Chinese from East China Normal University in Shanghai, and in 2000 received a PhD from Beijing's Tsinghua University, where he has taught literature ever since. He first started publishing short stories during the 1980s and quickly established himself as one of the most prominent writers of experimental avant-garde fiction in China. Ge Fei's scholarly publications include *Kafka's Pendulum* and his fiction includes the Jiangnan Trilogy and the novella *Flock of Brown Birds*. He was awarded the 2014 Lu Xun Literary Prize and the 2015 Mao Dun Prize for Fiction. *The Invisibility Cloak* is his first novel to be translated into English.

CANAAN MORSE is a translator, poet, and editor. He co-founded the literary quarterly *Pathlight: New Chinese Writing* and has contributed translations of Chinese prose and poetry to *The Kenyon Review*, *The Baffler*, and other journals. He is currently editing two anthologies of Chinese literature and translating a collection of the work of the Taiwanese poet Yang Xiaobin into English.

THE INVISIBILITY CLOAK

GE FEI

Translated from the Chinese by
CANAAN MORSE

NEW YORK REVIEW BOOKS

New York

Published by arrangement with People's Literature Publishing House Co., Ltd., China.

This book has been supported by 新闻出版广电总局 through the China Classics International Project

经典中国国际出版工程
China Classics International

Library of Congress Cataloging-in-Publication Data
Names: Ge, Fei, 1964– author. | Morse, Canaan, translator.
Title: The invisibility cloak / Ge Fei ; translated by Canaan Morse.
Other titles: Pi feng. English
Description: New York : NYRB Classics, 2016.
Identifiers: LCCN 2016011627 (print) | LCCN 2016024403 (ebook) | ISBN
  9781681370200 (paperback) | ISBN 9781681370217 (epub)
Subjects: LCSH: Divorced men—China—Fiction. | China—Social
  conditions—Fiction. | Psychological fiction. | BISAC: FICTION /
  Psychological. | FICTION / Literary. | FICTION / Crime. | GSAFD:
  Mystery fiction. | Suspense fiction.
Classification: LCC PL2872.F364 P513 2016 (print) | LCC PL2872.F364 (ebook) |
  DDC 895.13/52—dc23
LC record available at https://lccn.loc.gov/2016011627

ISBN 978-1-68137-020-0
Available as an electronic book; ISBN 978-1-68137-021-7

Printed in the United States of America on acid-free paper.
10 9 8 7 6 5 4 3 2 1

THE INVISIBILITY CLOAK

1. THE KT88

AT NINE a.m. sharp I pulled up to the Brownstones buildings. This residential complex sits on the eastern edge of the Winter Palace, with its northern face hugging the flyovers of the north Fifth Ring Road. "The Brownstones" has been a household name in Beijing for years, ever since they executed the district mayor, Zhou Liangluo, for accepting millions in bribes on local real estate deals, including the one that made these apartments. It was the first time I had ever been here. I had a client in Building 8 who had asked me to build a KT88 amplifier to boost his speakers, an Acapella bookshelf set. Acapella systems with Campanile horn speakers are a common enough sight in this city, their equalizers flickering with a ghostly blue light, but the shelf speakers I'd seen only in magazines. I worked day and night for two weeks to produce an amplifier that would fit the system, though whether or not it would produce a good sound was by no means certain.

The late autumn sky was beginning to clear after a night of rain, and visibility was so good it seemed you could reach out and touch the mist-curled trees of the Winter Palace, or the tall pagoda atop Baiwang Mountain. Another frost or two and the maples on the western mountains would start to turn. My mood, though, wasn't as cheerful as the weather. Five minutes ago I'd gotten a call from my sister,

Cui Lihua. My brother-in-law had gotten drunk last night, and kicked her in the "privates" with a square-toed leather shoe. This morning, she said, she'd had blood in her urine. The sound of her crying irritated me, and I simply stayed quiet on my end. It wasn't that I didn't feel like comforting her, but I sensed some other motive hidden behind her whimpering. Sure enough, after she'd gone on for a while, my sister said to me: "I can't take it anymore. Please, just move out. I don't want to live like this either. Have pity on me, as a brother to a sister. I'm begging you . . ."

I could hear both supplication and anger in my sister's voice as she wailed at me over the phone. As if it hadn't been that bastard Chang Baoguo who had kicked her, but me.

The security door for Unit 3 popped open. A woman in a gray athletic shirt leaned out from the doorway. She peered at me and at the mud-flecked minivan behind me, then finally caught sight of the KT88 at my feet. She smiled and gushed, "Oooh, it's so pretty!" I wasn't sure if she was being polite with her praise or slightly patronizing. The way she spoke reminded me of Yufen. Her face and form did too. I couldn't help but look her up and down a few times, as faint ripples of panic and sorrow crossed my heart. The KT88 amplifier I had worked so hard to build sat on the concrete stoop, its silver, velvety body shining in the morning sun.

Her husband had ordered the amplifier. I had met him at the International Hi-Fi Exhibition last October. I found him reserved, and a little annoying. I heard he was a professor, though I can't say of what, or at which university. He liked changing his mind. Initially he asked me to make him an EL34, but just as I was putting the final touches on the body, he called again, demanding that I switch over to the more powerful KT88.

The husband sat at his dining table, chatting with a friend over tea. He didn't pause in his conversation as I walked past him with the bulky KT88 in my arms, but merely acknowledged me with a stern nod. My experience dealing with professors has taught me that educated people have the ability to demean a person with a single glance. His friend didn't seem like your average guy either. A thick mustache guarded his mouth, making him look a little like Friedrich Engels.

The wife, in stark contrast, was quite friendly and asked if I preferred tea or coffee. Anything's fine, I replied, and sure enough, anything was what I received: she returned with a glass of orange soda. As I set up the speakers, she leaned over the back of the couch and quietly observed me. The more I looked at her, the more she reminded me of Yufen.

It was an easy job, not much for me to do. I installed a GEC KT88 electronic vacuum tube and an RCA 5u4 rectifier tube, verified its working amperage, then connected the lines for the signal and the horn speakers, and that was pretty much it. I noticed that the speaker boxes were placed a little too close to the wall and asked the hostess if we could change their location a little. Generally speaking, if the speaker is too close to a wall, the standing wave created in the ports will cause the lower registers to sound fuzzy; this is common knowledge. Yet before the woman could open her mouth, the professor turned his head around and yelled in a hostile tone: "Don't mess with anything!"

The woman looked at me, blinked, stuck out her tongue,

then said with a laugh, "Don't worry about it. He never lets anyone touch his stuff. How about we put on some music and try it out?"

"No rush; let's wait a moment first. I just plugged it in and the machine needs to preheat."

"Wow, so complicated!" Again, the half-curious, half-mocking tone.

I patiently explained that in order for the amplifier to produce the highest-quality sound, it had to be turned on for at least twenty minutes before use. She was a teacher as well, a volleyball instructor at the Beijing Sports Academy just up the road. With the help of a crude analogy, she immediately accepted the importance of "warming up."

As we waited, I flipped through their CD collection. All dated pop music—Mei Yanfang, Zhang Xueyou, and (of course) Cai Qin. Mostly pirated. I have no opinion when it comes to my clients' musical tastes. It doesn't matter to me if they like Renaissance, Baroque, or the Romantics, blues, jazz, or even "glass-shattering" heavy metal. But honestly, spending a hundred and fifty thousand yuan on an Acapella set so you can listen to pirated Mei Yanfang CDs seemed almost unbelievable. I realized with some consternation that I had been taking this job a little too seriously, spending two weeks fine-tuning the amp to perfection. If one really wants to listen to this kind of stuff, just spend five hundred yuan at the local electronics market on a pair of discount computer speakers.

Naturally, I didn't say any of this out loud, merely asked which CD she'd like to listen to. She said she didn't care. Their whole collection of "music" was organized right on the coffee table.

The professor and his friend were still talking in the dining room. For the most part, conversations between intellectuals are incomprehensible to the everyday person. Nothing strange or new about that, of course, yet their dead-serious tone of voice can enthrall nonetheless. With that tone, even the most ridiculous point of view sounds completely sensible. And so the Engels impersonator suddenly started to praise the Empress Dowager:

"Thank heavens she stole a percentage of the funds the navy was going to use to build destroyers and spent it on construction of the Summer Palace. When the war with the Japanese broke out, the ships would have been destroyed anyway. Thus we can see how corruption isn't always necessarily a bad thing. You can't help but admire the old Dowager's vision—after a little bit of work on her part, not only has she left us a World Heritage Site, just imagine the enormous sums of money we get per annum from ticket sales alone. I live outside the southwest corner of the palace; as long as it's not raining, I ride my bicycle through the grounds every day, in through the southern Gate of Fortune and out the North Palace Gate. Twenty years later, I'm still not tired of it."

The mention of the Empress Dowager jolted me to attention. My great-grandfather was once summoned to her court to perform Peking opera and received a gift of two bolts of silk in return. Listening to him stand up for her was comforting. Besides, I've always loved the Summer Palace myself, especially the landscape around the Jade Belt Bridge. Unfortunately, the tickets have grown more expensive with every passing year, and I hadn't been for nearly a decade. As for the Empress Dowager, my grandfather maintained his own judgment, which seemed to me a lot more objective than what Engels expressed. Even if she was quite intelligent, he once told me, she obviously didn't know much about the real world; in other words, she acted like nothing more than an average noblewoman of those times, penny-wise and pound-foolish. She mishandled an historical opportunity, and when it came down to saving the Qing dynasty or saving the country, she chose the former, with tragic results. When they nailed her to the historical whipping post, no one can say she didn't deserve it.

The professor listened to Engels' long pronouncement, nodding periodically. Yet his response was hardly credible. He expressed complete agreement with his friend's point of view; in fact, he saw the Sino-Japanese War itself as an unnecessary conflict. If, at the beginning of the war, China had surrendered directly, not only would it have saved hundreds of thousands of lives, but China and Japan could have joined forces to resist Western imperialism, which could have changed the global balance of power dramatically. Moreover, he had always felt that Wang Jingwei, the one-time president of the Japanese puppet government in Nanjing, was actually a national hero, no less than Li Hongzhang or Yuan Shikai, and that his life history should be thoroughly re-examined and his image rehabilitated. He even quoted a passage from Wang Jingwei's diary after the attack on Pearl Harbor.

The professor liked to repeat the rhetorical question "Am I right?" to emphasize his every point, as if he had merely to ask it and his nauseating opinions would be transmuted into truth. Though I don't consider myself an ardent nationalist, though I didn't have the skills to refute him, and though I've always respected intellectuals, his whole exhausting argument angered me. Why did his words have such an effect? What he said made me feel ashamed, like someone had just dug up my family's grave; I wanted to step forward and argue the point. What I found even more shocking as he blathered on about his admiration of Shintoism was that he pronounced the word for "spirits" as *shen-di*. Now, my formal education ended after one year at technical school and thus my knowledge of literature comes mostly from Xu Zhongyu's *College Level Language Arts*, but even I knew that word is pronounced *shen-qi* and not *shen-di*.

I tried my best to control myself, sliding out a copy of the opera *The Red Detachment of Women* to test out the sound. The professor's wife, however, requested a different CD. She liked Andy Lau. She said she almost shook Andy Lau's hand during his concert at the Worker's Stadium in 2004. I was in no position to argue with her. Still, you can imagine how I felt when lines like "give me a drink to forget your love" came drooling out of those beautiful Acapella speakers.

Goose bumps spread over my entire body; my mood dropped into my shoes.

I'm not saying that people shouldn't listen to Andy Lau. These days it just seems like everyone is listening to him, old and young, man and woman. I could rack my brain all night and never figure out why.

Something is definitely wrong with this world.

2. PEER GYNT

YOU ALREADY know that I build tube amplifiers for a living. If you counted the total number of people in Beijing who still make a living off this racket there wouldn't be more than twenty of us. It's probably the most insignificant industry in China today. The strange thing is that, although we're aware of each other's existence, we make a habit of keeping to ourselves. We don't overpraise each other, nor are we ever too critical of another's competence, careful not to undercut a fellow tradesman. Each protects his own dwindling group of clients and gets by as best he can. The vast majority of people in today's society seem totally oblivious to our existence. This isn't necessarily a bad thing. It gives us a good reason to look down on them, while finding dark corners in which to live self-sufficient, invisible lives.

The name "audiophile" has never sat well with me. I'm just a craftsman. It's something I've been proud of, truthfully, for many years. And you know that today's craftsmen more or less exist on the same rung of the social ladder as beggars. I'm sure certain deep, erudite intellectuals can provide a perfect explanation as to why Chinese society has changed so profoundly in this respect; but if you want a layman's take on it, I'd say the decline we're experiencing began with the deliberate humiliation of the craftsmen.

Still, there was a spell during the mid- to late nineties

when our industry boomed. Back then, the annual Beijing International Hi-Fi Exhibition overflowed with visitors, leaving you to wonder where all these fans of Bach and Wagner, and even of Wilhelm Furtwängler and Pablo Casals, could have come from. You did your business with men of taste and intelligence, and pop music was treated with universal contempt (which felt a little unfair, even to me). Everyone talked about western classical music, though if you wanted respect, you wouldn't mention Mozart or Beethoven. You discussed lesser-known composers, like Telemann, Mahler, or Giovanni Viotti. Today, people even consider Li Yuchun's ultralight pop tunes to be good music.

In those days, Beijing Radio 97.4 aired a show called "Audiophile Asylum." Every time it came on I would close my door, turn off the lights, and let myself fade into the darkness as I listened to it on my own personally built system. That was back in our old house on Mahogany Street. As the marvelous music permeated the dark night, the whole world seemed to fall silent at once, turning darkly mysterious. Even my two goldfish in their enameled stoneware basin would leap up and disturb the water with their tails, wriggling with cold excitement. An illusion of hiding in the quietest corner of the deepest place on earth would take over my consciousness.

Two years later, my custom amplifiers had generated an established clientele. I was even invited onto a call-in program on Beijing Radio as a guest "Hardware Doctor." And now? Not only has "Audiophile Asylum" long since signed off, just trying to find a classical music station on your car radio is harder than winning the lottery! Today's DJs seem to be more interested in talking—I'm not sure why. They babble on and on, sometimes punctuating their banter with fake laughter or applause, as if they were tickling themselves in front of the microphone. Pathetic.

In short, the kind of appreciation people had for classical music is unimaginable now. When my ex-wife (girlfriend at the time) was studying for her Associate's degree at Hebei Technical College, the school would play "Morning Mood" from Edvard Grieg's Peer Gynt Suite over the PA system as the morning wake-up call. Can you imagine what it must have felt like to wake up to the flutes and strings of that melody every day?

Now's as good a time as any as any to say something about my wife, Yufen. We met before I got started in the audio industry. I was selling shoes at Tong Sheng He, the famous shoe shop over on the main boulevard by the Wangfujing shopping street. I noticed her the moment she walked into the store. There was no way you couldn't notice her. She had that pure, perfectly formed face that gives you a feeling like a razor slash across the heart. How can I put it? You feel as if you'd risk your life just to be with her. She tried on three or four pairs of dress shoes without finding anything that fit her. She didn't buy anything, though she didn't leave either. She just sat all alone on the little leather stool and sighed to herself.

I had been watching her out of the corner of my eye for a while. It started getting dark outside, the flow of pedestrians on the street thinned, and the crows started to cackle in the trees lining the sidewalk. Closing time approached. I was worried about getting to the pharmacy in time to buy medicine for my mother, so I went over to her and asked in an authoritative tone: "Mind if I look at your feet?"

When your average person is faced with a tough problem, she naturally becomes open to suggestion and easy to influence. Yufen obediently raised her head and looked up at me, not at all taken aback by my abruptness. She pouted her lips and asked, "Which one do you want to see?"

"Either one's fine," I said.

She immediately took off her Puma sneakers and peeled off her nylon socks, which wasn't necessary. I took a look at her right foot, then turned around and grabbed two pairs of shoes off the rack behind me. She tried them on, and immediately decided to buy both pairs.

Before leaving, she asked me a question. She had been shoe shopping in Xidan and Wangfujing the whole day, and had tried on hundreds of pairs of shoes without finding anything she liked. Yet it only took me an instant to pick out two pairs for her that fit so well, it was as if they had been custom-made. How had I done it?

Maybe it was because I was in a good mood and feeling satisfied with myself that I waxed a little aphoristic in my response: "Oh, that's not surprising. People are always choosing things that don't fit them."

Looking back at the way things panned out, that innocent remark was more like an omen. The next time Yufen came in to buy shoes, I asked her out to dinner at the duck restaurant across from the Children's Theater. She accepted. A week later, I took her to a movie. She was very easygoing, so much so it almost made me nervous. I could never figure this out about her. Like I was observing her through a fog. We didn't fight once in the first two years of our relationship, nor did she ever get sharp with me about anything. It was as if she had been put on this earth solely to please other people, or at least me.

My best friend, Jiang Songping, once lamented that Beijing girls all possessed a bit of the tough bitch in them, ready to slap a man with a shoe at the slightest tremor of displeasure. Seems he was wrong about that one. I took Yufen over to his place once; he was bewildered, even a little annoyed at my "good luck." Whenever he talked to her, even in my presence, his body would unconsciously tilt forward.

I guess "falling for someone" isn't just an expression after all.

By the end of the nineties, I had saved up some money from making amplifiers. With this small measure of financial security, I immediately quit my job at Tong Sheng He, rented a stall in the Superwave Audio Mall (still a one-floor courtyard back then), and worked for a Hong Kong franchise that sold Tannoy speakers made in Britain. You'd have had a hard time not making money at the audio market in Beijing back then. It wasn't long before I bought a two-bedroom apartment north of the city center in Shangdi. Finally figuring I was ready to propose, I took Yufen back home to meet my mother. Honestly, what I wanted most was for my mother to be proud of me.

By that time Ma already knew what she was sick with, but she still retained her sense of humor during conversation. I brought Yufen into my mother's room to show her off real quick before asking if she could go help my sister with dinner. Alone, I sat down at Ma's bedside and, feeling sure of myself, asked if she was happy with the daughter-in-law I had brought home.

The old lady considered it for a long time, then took my

hand and squeezed it, saying, "Well, this little one has the right lines to her."

Definitely not what I wanted or expected to hear. What did she mean by "the right lines"? It sounded odd, like something you'd say when appraising a litter of piglets fresh from the pen. Another pause, then my mother wheezed and continued: "This one has a good temper. And she has kindness and compassion in her character."

A weight lifted from me. I was wholly convinced that she was praising Yufen, which, you know, made me happier than anything. Ma lay there, body bent to one side. After a spasmodic fit of coughing, she patted the edge of the bed, beckoning me to sit beside her. How could I have imagined that she would put a hand on my arm and say, "Son, if my opinion doesn't matter to you, then ignore me. But if you really want to hear your mother's advice, I'll tell you: I think it's best if you don't marry her. When she entered, I read her face—everything about her seems fine, but she has no hatch marks to her."

I asked her what she meant by "no hatch marks." Ma was a southerner, born in Yancheng, Jiangsu province, and her Mandarin was always mixed with her local dialect, making it very hard to understand her sometimes. She thought for a moment, then replied, still smiling, "She's just a little too easy come, easy go. It's not a good thing. To put it bluntly: you're marrying this woman for somebody else. A family like ours can't afford it."

She followed her advice with an old rhyme: "Look at her from head to toes, downward the easy spirit flows; look at her from toes to head, the easy rises up instead." I couldn't help but laugh.

Still, on National Day, the day I married Yufen, Ma

didn't say anything. She didn't object, didn't show any sign of displeasure. When my sister led the new bride to her bedside to bow and call her "Ma," my mother responded energetically, and even pushed herself into a sitting position to return the courtesy. Then she placed into Yufen's hands the ceremonial red envelope that contained two hundred yuan she had been saving under her pillow for who knows how long, and gave Yufen a hug.

Four years have passed since my mother's prediction came true.

One day, Yufen came home from work and asked me sweetly for a divorce. Apparently, she had "gotten together" with the new director at her office. Two packs of cigarettes out on the balcony couldn't console me. I walked straight into the darkness of our bedroom and shook her awake, begging her in a whisper to "think about it some more." Yufen blinked and replied, half asleep, "Think about what? Honey, we're already doing it."

There was nothing I could do but walk into the kitchen and drive a fruit knife into the back of my hand.

The period of our divorce happened around the time of my mother's death. Everyone who knew her—neighbors, old colleagues, and friends—had pleaded with her to go to the hospital. Ma refused outright. She would only look at them and smile. She had made her own calculations. She knew that once she went into the hospital, there was no way she was coming out. That, and she didn't want to spend the money. In the end, my uncle had to make the trip all the way up from Yancheng to argue with her before she finally allowed us to admit her.

For the eleven days she lasted in the hospital, I visited her a few times at her bedside, not staying for more than five minutes. Yufen's infidelity put me in a bad emotional state. My sister, Cui Lihua, knew what was going on.

"But our mom's going to *die*!" she yelled at me, stamping her foot.

"I wouldn't mind dying myself, you know!" I replied.

She saw how foul my mood was and left me alone. She sat at our mother's bedside every night, and in the mornings commuted to the sewage treatment plant in Shijingshan where she worked. Dark circles appeared around her eyes; she seemed to be constantly glaring. Meanwhile, my bastard brother-in-law, Chang Baoguo, was already bad-mouthing me to friends and relatives. There was nothing I could do about that.

The last time I saw my mother in the hospital, she was heavily drugged and slipping in and out of consciousness. Not wanting to disturb her rest, I shot my sister a look, stood at the bedside for a minute and turned to leave. But my mother opened her eyes and called my name.

She insisted on sending my sister home and keeping me there.

"Just for one night, okay?" she asked with a smile.

Of course I couldn't refuse.

For me to stay awake the whole night by her bedside, however, wasn't really necessary. She was lucid only for short moments. Each time she woke, she asked me turn her on her side so she could look at me, which, honestly, made me really uncomfortable. Ma had a small frame to begin with, and the disease had shrunk her even more. Once in a while, she would take my hand and rub the back of it gently—her expression tranquil, even a faint trace of a smile. She saved up her energy through the night, and just as the sun was about to rise, she said everything she needed to say.

The hospital must have been near a military barracks because I remember the clear call of reveille being played as dawn broke. Of course, it wasn't Peer Gynt. Ma said she knew her time was near, if not today then most likely tomorrow. It hurt a lot to hear her say it. She already knew from my sister about my divorce from Yufen. She didn't scold me for not listening to her, but simply said:

"Back then, I told you not to marry her, didn't I? Well, you didn't listen, and I didn't press it. A girl like that, pretty as a picture, I could tell that she was all you could see. If I'd stepped in and tried to stop you, who knows if you'd have been able to stand the strain. So I said to myself, it's fine, get married and we'll see. If it really doesn't work, we can get a divorce, then find someone else and marry again. Heaven gives you no dead ends, as they say; sometimes, right when you think you can't take it, you just grit your teeth and put your head down, and suddenly you're through. And it wasn't such a big deal in the first place. I'll tell you one thing, and don't you forget it: everyone has a wife waiting for him somewhere. It's fate, the way the world works. If it's not Yufen, it's somebody else. Where is she? I don't know, and there's no use in you scouring heaven and earth looking for her. Before the time is right, you'll never find her; when it is, she'll be right there in front of you, ready to give you a family. It's not that I'm superstitious, you'll see; it will happen. Keep an open mind, and when the time comes, you'll know. You'll see her and you'll think to yourself, Oh, there she is …"

I interrupted her. "You know, it's funny; that's exactly what I thought when I first saw Yufen."

Ma chuckled and licked her dry lips. "That's called infatuation!"

"But what if I meet the woman I'm supposed to be with and don't recognize her? What do I do?"

Ma pondered this for a while, an unexpected tear running down each cheek. After a prolonged pause, she said, "Ridiculous child, do you want me to visit you in a dream when the time comes?"

Outside, a steady rain pelted the windows. My mother took her deposit book out from underneath her pillow. She put it in my hand and curled my fingers into a fist. She held that fist in both hands and squeezed hard. Her entire life's savings was in that account. She instructed me to not tell Lihua no matter what.

I didn't shed a single tear at my mother's funeral. I hurt as much as the rest of them, but I just couldn't cry. I didn't know what was wrong with me. At the wake, while Chang Baoguo and the others howled and wailed at the top of their lungs, I still couldn't cry. I was harboring a secret, turning a question over and over in my mind: should I tell Lihua about the deposit account? I didn't actually care that much about twenty-seven thousand yuan. I just couldn't gauge how Lihua and Baoguo would react if I told them. Lihua took responsibility for our mother immediately after she got sick, yet Ma sent Lihua away the night before she died and gave the account book to me. Whether or not this would make Lihua and Baoguo hysterical at the funeral, I couldn't tell.

After Yufen divorced me, I moved out of my place in Shangdi and into an apartment my sister owned in Shijing-shan. It was a nice building, part of a new utility housing project she had applied for through her work unit. Not long after I moved in, I noticed a large crack had opened in the north wall of the living room. It kept things nice and cool in the summer, but when winter arrived, three full rolls of tape weren't enough to keep the wind and sand out. My sister and I once paid a visit to the building offices to kick up a fuss. The representatives laughed, saying that settling soil created intolerable stress on the walls and that it was a global problem. They shooed us away. Still, it was probably the crack and the draft that had caused Chang Baoguo and my sister to move into my mother's old place on Mahogany Street. I thought to myself: You know, that living room wall couldn't have picked a better time to split.

Yufen dropped by some time after that. Her new man, the director, had made a mistake while he was debugging a numerical control machine tool they had imported from Germany; he jammed it and blew out one of the components on the circuit. The machine wasn't cheap; if the Board found out, he probably wouldn't be director any more. I had used machine tools back in the day when I was making custom boxes for transistor amplifiers; and so Yufen suddenly appeared in the middle of the night to ask me to look at it for her.

Naturally, I refused.

Like I said, I'm fairly expert with anything related to sound systems, and if you asked me to fix an AC unit or a personal computer or something, I could probably figure it out. But this was a large-scale, imported numerical control machine tool—I had never even seen one before. Yufen thought I was backing down out of insecurity, and said, "Oh, please. Calling it an imported machine tool makes it sound so mysterious or whatever, but it's not necessarily any more complicated than those computers and amplifiers you sell. Besides, you're the patron saint of mechanics. Machines fear you. They intentionally make problems for the rest of us, but with you it's different. Who knows, maybe it'll hear your footsteps and get so scared that it fixes itself."

Hearing her say that made me feel pretty good. In the end, I couldn't resist her flattery and insistent pleading and agreed to take a look. Of course, I met her new husband, Director Luo. He followed me around with a stack of German instruction manuals, talking incessantly. I finally got angry enough to ask him to back off and be quiet. He didn't get offended, just stood there and giggled.

It was my first encounter with a machine of that scale, and I spent a full four hours trying to figure out its operating principles. After that, finding and fixing the problem only took about twenty minutes. I realized that Yufen must have lied to Director Luo about our history. When they took me out to eat afterward, he asked me very politely where I lived and how old my children were. He said that if my kids ever wanted to study in Germany, just ask him.

Yufen paid me another visit a few days later. My mother's assessment of her character had been right. Yufen was still attracted to me. She smiled slyly and asked if all this living alone was hard to bear. She offered to help me "take a load off." I wasn't about to offend her good intentions with a snub. I discovered she was already pregnant; you can imagine how that burned. While we were doing it, she wouldn't stop complimenting me, saying that I was just as good at handling women as I was machines. Her husband, a returned immigrant from Munich, apparently was better looking than he was in bed. By the time he got her hot and ready to roll, he became as soft and shriveled as a paraplegic. She hadn't had a single orgasm in the four months they'd been married. I didn't know if I should feel happy or hurt.

We had one more illicit rendezvous after that. But I

guess a guy like me just doesn't have the nerve to keep up such a relationship. When we were together, the image of Luo's boyish face kept floating in my mind. I couldn't silence a gnawing feeling of guilt. So I steeled myself and said to Yufen: "We're divorced. Since you're now married to this Mr. Luo, you should go back and be with him like you're supposed to, instead of coming around here. I can't deal with it. Your Mr. Luo looks like an educated, civilized guy, better than I am in every way. Your orgasms aren't more important than that. The two of us can't carry on like this. Besides, now that you're pregnant, it's not a good idea. You shouldn't come back here any more."

Yufen had a wrenched expression on her face as I walked her to the subway. She held it together for a while, but then she wrapped her arms around me and started to cry. What she told me next I thought about for at least two months afterward. She said the first time she had gotten together with someone else wasn't with Luo but with some dirty maintenance worker. Once, during a night shift, he had cornered her in the bathroom and they had gone crazy in a toilet stall.

Yufen never came back to Shijingshan. And I never listened to the Peer Gynt Suite she liked so much ever again. I did see her once more—in Sanlitun, on my way to Dongdaqiao to fix an LP turntable for a client. Tables with umbrellas were arranged in a line under the heavy shade of trees outside a café. She sat sipping her drink with a black guy, who had one hand on her smooth shoulder.

I didn't dare say hello.

3. THE NURSERY RECORD

AFTER finishing the job at the Brownstones that morning, I made a run to the Ping'anli Electronics Market. I picked up a roll of WBT silver solder, a couple of salvaged Dutch oil-filled capacitors, and a pair of Nordost "Red Dawn" signal cables. As I already had a pair of the cables at home, these completed the set. On my way home to Shijingshan that afternoon, I stopped by Golden Square near Seasons Bridge to see my old friend Jiang Songping.

Generally speaking, my clients can be divided into two groups. The first group, as you already know, is mainly made up of intellectuals. Most of them live in the Haidian district, near the universities. Their good qualities are courtesy, politeness, and punctual payment. They almost never pay late, and sometimes, when money is tight for me, they'll even be willing to put up a deposit in advance. People of their sort tend to want amplifiers that bring out the feeling or color of the music—the so-called "musical flavor." They're very irregular customers, and their numbers have been shrinking every year. Dealing with them involves learning how to endure their pontificating. To be fair, there are times when high-minded discourse can really open your eyes; other times, it will only drive you insane. They all bear the same sanctimonious expression on their faces, as if the fate of the world lay securely in their hands. Going by my own inexpert observations, their opinions are actually pretty inconsistent.

For instance, there's a handful of professors who love to warn me every time we meet that a society like China's could collapse at any moment. I've never once brought the subject up myself, yet they still seize every opportunity to sit at their dining tables and guide my understanding. I end up having nightmares. They've been repeating the same thing for a good ten or twenty years now. One year passed; five years, twenty years have passed; and the sun's still hanging right up there in the sky! China continues on, as fine as can be; nothing cataclysmic has happened.

Then there's another handful who take the exact opposite position. They believe China is right at the zenith of her history, and that the whole world is gazing up at us in admiration. Everywhere else, the world is in crisis and people look desperately to China for salvation, while we're rolling in so many billions of shiny dollar bills, we don't know who to save first—should it be Iceland or Greece, Italy or America? I'm not sure what the actual situation really is. I'd rather leave it to the politicians and the academics. Anyway, it doesn't take them long to confuse me.

My other groups of clients, of course, are business owners of varying degrees of wealth. At first glance, you'd think men like these, with their fat wallets and empty souls, would be the last to have any connection to real classical music. The fact that they've become steady sources of income for me has been made possible solely through Jiang Songping's recommendations and introductions. Songping calls it "fishing," and his strategy never changes.

Whenever Songping hosts a party or a private get-together at his house, it frequently involves bringing his partners, board members, or whoever else is present on a mandatory tour of his basement, which boasts a nearly sixty-square-meter home theater. The sound system it uses is both brilliantly functional and aesthetically beautiful: Amati Anniversario speakers by the Italian company Sonus Faber, their wood lacquered and buffed to the tones of a violin and a mirror's shine; a McIntosh 50th anniversary commemorative edition amplifier, with green and blue lights that flicker on the face when you turn it on; a Nagra CD console, as carefully designed as a Swiss watch, with a first-class Clearandio LP turntable sitting on top. In terms of sound quality, the system pays attention to detail and differentiation.

At one point during the tour (usually after ten o'clock at night, as Songping almost never listens to music before ten; he claims that only at night is there stable enough voltage and a clean enough current to create beautiful music), Songping will put a finger to his lips and hush everyone softly, then turn on the blue wall lighting. The walls of the basement have all been lined with a special egg-crate sound-proofing material. He will draw down a heavy cashmere curtain, don a pair of white gloves, and tiptoe into the maze of boxes and electrical cables. He will take a CD from the pile on the coffee table, a disc we call the "Nursery Record," spritz its underside with a cleaning agent, and wipe it dry with mirror cloth. The whole ordeal seems more like leading his guests in a ritual performance rather than simply playing them music.

Although the dust in Beijing can get a little severe, I still caution him against using chemical cleaners on his CDs.

There's always a chance the agent in the fluid will erode the plastic surface of the disc and interfere with the tracking. Frankly, the best cleaner you can use is pure water. Songping never listens. He always gives me the same irrational answer: "Are you kidding? This is no ordinary cleaner. You know I buy this stuff specially imported from England? You know how many pounds a bottle this size costs? Take a fucking guess. Use water? You're kidding me."

So I shut my mouth again.

As the music from the Nursery Record unrolls like bolts of silk, some of the well-fed executives whose brains are as full as their bellies will lean into the leather couch and begin to snore. But that's no problem—there are always a few among them who take the bait. They succumb to the charm of the Nursery Record. Looks of amazement appear on their faces, like they can't believe their own ears. Their eyes glow green with envy, and they nod repeatedly, as if listening to heaven's melodic strains.

More often than not, before the end of the first movement, someone stands up and announces decisively, "No wonder Songping is so obsessed with music he doesn't even grab girls' asses any more. I see the light! Songping, get me one exactly like yours, quick! I want it now!"

One such announcement is enough to keep me busy for months, and five or six of these "victims" a year is enough to keep my pathetic business hobbling along. I buy the speaker boxes, cables, and CD players from the secondhand markets or off eBay, and then I secretly install my own custom amplifiers into the system. I only charge for the amplifiers. Of course, the systems I build for them can't possibly be exactly like Jiang Songping's. But you can bet the Nursery Record that hooked them in the first place is a mandatory freebie.

I might as well say a bit more about the Nursery Record.

It's a very well-known recording, originally cut as an LP by Decca in 1962, then remastered for CD in 1993. The music was composed by a Frenchman named Hérold, born at the end of the eighteenth century. It was originally written as the score for an opera about a group of young women during the French Revolution, and their longing for independence. The title was originally translated as something like "The Wayward Girl." Later, the music was arranged for orchestra by a man named Lanchbery, who conducted it himself in a performance by the Orchestra of the Royal Opera House at Covent Garden. As for the original composer, Hérold, he may well be a complete nobody, someone you could flip through every musical dictionary looking for and never find. But to a lot of newcomers to classical music, this recording of his work has worked like a drug. Its tone color, sense of space, and orchestral richness evoke a kind of yin-yang beauty of strength and softness working in concert with each other. I don't even like the tune very much, but I still must admit that it sets a truly unsurpassable standard for performance and recording. If you had never heard any classical music before in your life, it would only take five or six minutes of patient listening to this album before you gave in completely to its allure. You'd think you had fallen in love with "classical music." It's all a delusion, of course. It's because this record has brought so many people over the threshold of classical music that it earned the title of the "Nursery Record."

Pretty much every one of the hi-fi enthusiasts I knew owned a copy. And escorting friends into his basement to listen to it became Jiang Songping's prestige performance. He didn't do it just to help me "fish" for clients, either. He played the violin in college, listened to Jascha Heifetz and Leonid Kogan, and enjoyed showing off his highbrow tastes to his friends.

In addition to Songping's endless flow of friends and guests, his wife had a whole battery of relations on her side who loved to gather at their house. I don't remember the place ever being quiet. "Seats always filled, cups never empty," as the saying goes. Like having dinner would be impossible with fewer than seventeen or eighteen guests present. Their home was one constant holiday party.

And this day, too, would be no exception.

The post-luncheon living room had recovered its original tidy state, but the air was still heavy with the scents of grain alcohol, peppercorn, and Sichuan sausage. A group of women sat attentively among the couches, listening to an eight- or nine-year-old girl play the violin. I didn't recognize a single one of them. Still seated at the table were two withered, expressionless old women, both so decrepit that it was all they could do to keep breathing. One of them was Jiang Songping's aunt, the other his mother-in-law. They sat in silence, casting occasional blank glances in our direction.

The little girl played Rachmaninoff's "Vocalise," and after being pressed by the crowd, played "Spring in Xinjiang." She was awful, I must say. After a while I had a hard time feigning interest, so I got up and went down to the basement.

I couldn't find Songping there either. I could make out the forms of a few people in the darkness watching *Pirates of the Caribbean* with 3D glasses on. The maid, coming

down with a plate of fruit, told me that Songping was upstairs in his study.

He wasn't alone. A middle-aged man in a coffee-colored
traditional Chinese jacket sat across from him at his desk.
Too much alcohol had turned him beet red from his neck
all the way up to his veiny forehead. Songping introduced
him to me as Master Hang, a renowned geomancer. He was
planning to build a new clothing factory in the suburbs of
Daxing and had invited Master Hang to look at the land
for him. It was rumored that this multitalented adept could
read fortunes as well as landscapes. Songping pressed him
to tell my fortune; I wasn't in a position to refuse. Master
Hang forced his bleary eyes open and shook his head violently back and forth as if to tear himself from a stupor.
Then he turned to me with an ingratiating smile and asked
what aspect of my fortune I would like to know about. He
slipped Songping an inebriated look, mumbling, "No,
wait . . . I think I'm going to hurl."

"Look at his love life for him," Songping offered. "My
buddy doesn't have any vices, he just worries all the time
about getting married."

Master Hang reached into his shirt pocket and pulled
out three bronze coins, the imperial-era kind with the hole
in the middle, already worn lustrous from use. He put the
coins into my hand and told me to make the toss. I threw
them six times onto the carpet as he instructed. The Master
dry-heaved a few times, then asked Songping for pen and
paper. He drew a couple lines, his eyes rolled back in his
head, and he proclaimed, "Already been married."

Then the Master closed his oracular mouth and fell into
a mystical silence. This particular fortune had apparently

come to a close. In a quiet voice, I asked if he could explain what he meant by "already been married." The Master paid no attention to me, instead turning to stare at Songping with a look of uncertainty in his drunken eyes.

"No . . . definitely gonna hurl."

With his hands on the desk, he pushed himself unsteadily to his feet and let out two long, squealing farts. Disgust spread across Songping's face, probably motivated by anxiety over the Master staining his carpet. He motioned him downstairs, and the Master hurried off with one hand over his mouth.

I said to Songping, "His utterance just now: 'already been married.' I don't understand it."

"He means you're done," Songping replied. "Sounds like you should just forget about getting married in this lifetime. So now why not stop worrying about that lowlife bitch Rayray—"

Here he was cut off by the sound of vomiting rising out from his flower garden. The Master retched with such volume and force that even Songping couldn't keep from grimacing.

The "Rayray" Songping mentioned was Zhu Ruirui, a former cashier at his company. After my divorce, Songping started setting me up on dates. But the women he found for me were either pudgy servers from the worker's cafeteria or thick-skinned cleaning ladies from the janitor's office. Not one I could even begin to like. Songping assumed the job of finding me a woman as a personal responsibility. The two of us grew up together, and we knew each other well. Besides him, I can't really think of anyone I could really call a "friend." Whenever he complained that I was too picky, I would solemnly remind him that just because I was poor didn't mean I couldn't have standards. Rayray the cashier caught my eye, though; she had a cute, giggly laugh, and her eyes reminded me of Yufen's. Once, when Songping and I were drunk, I indirectly expressed my intentions to him. He reacted with fright, gave an equivocating laugh, and asked, "What do you see in her?"

I told him what my mother said to me on her deathbed, about every man on earth having a wife somewhere, hiding in a corner of the world, and when the time was right she would appear right in front of him, that as soon as you saw her, you'd know this was the woman heaven and earth had appointed for you. The first time I saw Zhou Ruirui, I said, that was exactly how I felt.

Songping considered this for a moment, then said definitively, "No way. You can choose anyone else in the factory except for her."

Not many days later, Jiang Songping helped Zhu Ruirui move to Ottawa and gain Canadian citizenship. She even bore him a son. You can imagine why I felt angry, and a little dirty, whenever I saw Songping after that. To make it worse, in conversations with me he started to refer to her as "your cousin." I felt so betrayed that I even swore I'd never talk to him again. But fate comforted me eventually. Less than two years after she got to Canada, Zhu Ruirui ran off with a drummer. Songping couldn't even get visitation rights. Gradually, we could talk about her openly, as if talking about a stranger.

The Master didn't come back upstairs after his vomiting fits. Songping plucked a cigar from a wooden box. He put it in his mouth and gently positioned the other end over the flame of his torch lighter.

"There's something important I want to talk to you

about. I've recently made a new friend. What he does, where's he's from, I have no idea. Seriously, I don't know much about him. But when you meet him in person, he gives you this—how do I put it—there's just something eerie about him. I don't know why; he looks totally ordinary. But there's something about the expression on his face that's fucking terrifying. I'm not going to lie to you—in the circles where the real money moves, I'm a nobody. You know that. But I asked around, and nobody could tell me who he is, where he's from. His name is weird, too: Ding Caichen. Hey, did you ever see that old horror flick *Her Lost Soul*? Well, anyway...this guy, this Mr. Ding, we became acquainted a few days ago through a mutual friend. He told me I absolutely had to help him acquire the highest-quality sound system in the world. The more extravagant the better. Obviously money isn't an issue. Not a bad deal, right? OK. The first person I thought of was you."

"Does he listen to hi-fi?"

"Doesn't seem like it." Songping's expression shifted slightly—talking about this man put fear in his eyes. "He's a big fish, that's for sure, but you need to be careful. If you try to stick it to him, don't go overboard. In situations like these, it's always better to leave yourself a little wiggle room. My gut tells me this guy's not entirely on the level."

"Will he pay in advance?"

"You can work that out with him. Here's his card. Just give him an account number and have him wire you the deposit. But you need to watch your back when you're dealing with the likes of him. I don't know what it is, but when he looks at you his gaze is like ice, like there's nothing behind his eyes. He's one of those people that makes chills go down your spine from the moment you see him."

For Songping to have met this guy only once and still be so horrified by him probably seems a little hard to believe, even to you, right? And right then, while I might have been a little curious about this new client, I didn't dwell on the possibility.

I had skipped lunch and trekked to Songping's place because I had another problem on my mind.

My sister, Cui Lihua, had given me an ultimatum: move out of her apartment at once. I had just gotten off the phone with her, giving in to her demand. As she pushed me to my emotional limit, the image of Songping's well-fed face floated into view. It gave me security. So I gritted my teeth and agreed. I thought how, after forty-eight years of fighting on this earth, I was finally about to become homeless; an uncontrollable pang of hopelessness and fatigue pierced my chest.

I asked Songping if he could make some space for me somewhere in the clothing factory, just so I could have a place to lay my head for a while. It didn't matter where it was: a garage, a warehouse, wherever. Songping looked at me with surprise, then he picked up his cell phone from the charger on his desk and started rifling through texts, one by one. He pulled one corner of his mouth into an unnatural smile.

"I still don't understand. I thought you were doing fine over there in Shijingshan. What makes you so eager to move?"

"The apartment's my sister's. She's pretty hard up herself. She plans to rent it out."

"If I remember correctly, there's a huge hole in the north wall of that old apartment, wind howling in and so on. How could she possibly rent it?"

"My sister and brother-in-law want to move back to Shijingshan themselves and rent out the old courtyard home on Mahogany Street. Some executive from a securities firm approached them, says he wants to turn the place into a bar."

"And how's your mother's health?" Songping suddenly asked.

"She passed away five, no, six years ago now." It was my turn to look surprised.

"That's right, you told me before. Look at me, my brain's like a sieve these days. When your memory goes, it goes all at once. I was in Canada when your mother passed away, and not being able to make it to the funeral makes it feel like she's still alive. I remember back when we were little, living there on Mahogany Street, I'd get hungry and she'd give me some of her fried sticky-rice cakes. So flaky and crisp. Your house was right down the street, yeah, with a courtyard, too? Open a bar in a location like that and you'd never lack business."

A pause. Songping sighed gently, and went on: "I don't have any free space for you here. You know what business has been like at the factory these last couple years. We make brand-name shirts and sell them overseas, and we barely get enough back to cover labor expenses. The economy is bad everywhere, Europe and America, and I'm sitting on a huge stockpile of product. And the workers today are constantly hungry for more; salaries go up, benefits go up, I can't absorb it all."

"I won't stay long. Two months, maybe, six at the longest. As soon as I find a decent place, I'll move out."

Songping didn't reply, but turned to look out the west-facing window. "The temperature's starting to drop. The maple trees in the mountains aren't fully red yet, but they're starting to turn. This morning, when I woke up and looked out the window, I thought I was still in Canada."

"They want me to move out by the end of the month. I can talk to my sister, but her husband, Chang Baoguo, is the main problem. He's from Hubei and has a short temper. He'll spit right into your collar if he gets mad enough. He's a taxi driver. Got into a bad accident up in Changping last year. He killed the other driver, and ended up handicapped himself."

"People from Hubei can be hard to deal with. Smart as a nine-headed hydra, they say." Songping passed me a small cup of black tea and smiled: "Yesterday someone sent me a little 'Yunnan Red.' Have a taste. Everybody's been buying 'Golden Forelock' nowadays, and the price has become a bit unreasonable. But I've always thought the flavor of 'Yunnan Red' better anyway."

"Chang Baoguo usually doesn't bother me, but he takes it out on my sister almost every day. I feel bad staying in that apartment. This morning he kicked her in the...under her stomach with a square-toed leather shoe. She's been pissing blood."

"When the cart gets to the foot of the mountain, a path will appear," Songping quoted. His face darkened and he frowned again. "I need to use the bathroom."

When he returned from the bathroom, he was wearing athletic sweats and a windbreaker. He stuffed a paper bag into my hand and told me he was going to a club on Fragrant Hill to play tennis. Then, as if he'd just remembered something, he said, "Remember to call that guy Ding up. How you do business with him is your affair, but there's just one thing: whatever you have to say, say it, without asking too many questions."

All I could do was excuse myself and go. If you had caught sight of me at that moment, you wouldn't have missed the look of desperation and shame on my face. As I turned to leave, Songping stopped me. He asked me to wait for a second.

Leaning on his desk and playing with his extinguished cigar, he stared at me with a strange expression, a smile that wasn't a smile.

"I want to remind you of something. It might not be my place to say it, but don't take it personally," he said quietly.

"If you have something to say, say it, and stop wasting time." I was starting to get agitated. His changing the subject just now had unsettled me.

"Don't take your sister's ultimatum too seriously; it's really an empty threat."

"What the hell are you talking about?"

"Your sister is obviously lying to you."

"I don't..."

"You just said that this morning, your brother-in-law Chang Baoguo kicked her in the stomach with a square-toed shoe, right? Well, think about it: where the hell would you get a square-toed leather shoe these days? You've sold shoes before, you should know better than me. What's more, if your brother-in-law lost the use of a leg after the accident in Changping, well, then it wouldn't matter which leg he supported himself with," here Songping waved a hand over his crotch area, "he'd never be able to kick that high. So, either your sister is lying, or..."

Then he gave a knowing smile, gazing at me like some kind of cocky amateur detective. The self-satisfied expression on his face truly irritated me. Of course I knew what he was implying.

He thought that I might be the one lying.

By the time I got back to my car, a light drizzle was coming down. I opened the paper bag and looked inside: a couple of new Tommy Hilfiger shirts. It wasn't the first time Songping had given me shirts. Still, as I looked down at this particular pair with their crosshatched design, I don't why, but I felt an incredible sadness.

4. THE SHORTWAVE RADIO

ON FRIDAY morning, I got another call from my sister, this time inviting me over for dinner at the Mahogany Street house. She would make pork-and-fennel dumplings for me. Although I'm a native Beijinger, I don't really like dumplings, especially not ones with fennel in them. My sister said that Chang Baoguo had been in a good mood ever since he heard that I'd agreed to move out. He hadn't kicked her again, and he wanted to sit down and have a few drinks with me. I bought some fruit and also brought along the two Tommy Hilfiger shirts as gifts for the hosts. I didn't dare tell them where the shirts came from. The name Jiang Songping was taboo in our house and had been for many years, repressed along with a certain story from our childhood.

Whether or not Chang Baoguo knew the story I wouldn't presume.

I hadn't been back to the family home since my mother's death. I passed right by it once, on my way to the open market by Red Gate Bridge to buy KR amplifier tubes from a Fujianese guy. From a ways off I could see that the courtyard door was shut, so I decided not to bother them. Their son lives in the south, in Shenzhen, and apparently can't be bothered to keep in touch with his parents. They made the long journey there to visit him once, but this nephew of mine, who apparently married a Malaysian woman and works as a top executive at some corporation, refused to see them. So they went to the Window of the World theme park, snapped some bad pictures in front of miniature replicas of the Arc de Triomphe and Dutch windmills, then hastened back to Beijing with their tails between their legs.

Yet that never discouraged my sister from bragging about her successful son to everyone she met.

Mahogany Street is just like every other narrow *hutong* alley in the south part of Beijing. Some people call it Mahogany Lane, others the Armory, most likely referring to a time when the area was known for its foundries that manufactured armor for Manchu soldiers. It's a historic neighborhood, at any rate. Our house originally consisted of two cramped brick rooms. We built an additional room when my father was still alive. Later, the district development committee started to come around regularly, trying to enforce a removal order for redevelopment. My father never gave them a word of response. Even when pressed hard, he would simply express his opinion with one long sigh: "Ah!"

But no one could ever figure out what the hell he meant by "Ah!"

After a while, my mother started to crack under the pressure; my father, however, decided to push back even harder. He used the bricks left over from the renovation to wall off a courtyard in front of the house at least thirty square meters wide. Shockingly, after he did it, the development committee stopped showing up. They expressed their tacit acceptance, perhaps afraid of my father's reticence.

My father was tall, pale-skinned, and a little stooped. He was indifferent to almost everything. He used to work full-time at a state-owned factory near Jiuxian Bridge that made radio tubes, but somehow managed to get laid off. After that he spent his days in a white apron and blue canvas sleeve protectors, fixing radios in a workshop one street down from our house. I was still a kid then. One day I asked my mother why my father never talked to us. Because he's sad, my mother replied, and it's changed him. She told me that when I was still a baby, the first thing he would do when he came home from work every day was to run inside without even taking his boots off and kiss me all over my face. When my mother said this, Cui Lihua looked up at her with an uncertain expression.

"Did he kiss me too?" my timid older sister asked, unable to keep it in any longer.

My mother thought for a moment, then smiled and mussed my sister's hair. "You too," she said. "He kissed you, too."

A day finally arrived when, in that dark little shop, my father lay down at his workstation amid a pile of semiconductors and died, still clutching a small green screwdriver in one hand.

They said he had a coronary.

That evening I arrived early. Chang Baoguo was out playing cards at a neighbor's place. My sister stood at the kitchen counter, chopping meat. She had some ground pork in the fridge she could have cooked but said that machine-ground meat tasted of metal. Though only two years older than me, she showed her age more severely. It was the first time in many years that I'd looked at her closely. There was something ingratiating about her expression whenever she smiled. It had always been there, but now, staring at her face inspired a twinge of loathing. She asked me if I had met anyone I liked recently, then followed up immediately with the announcement that she had a colleague in the office who was divorced, in her forties, had a boy of about thirteen, you know, a nice, straightforward person, "pretty and well-proportioned," with just a slight lisp when she talked, did I want to meet her?

I told her that a couple days ago I had run into a fortune teller, and from his pronouncement it seemed I should forget about getting married in this life. Of course I didn't mention where I had bumped into him; she would still have no desire to hear the name "Jiang Songping."

"You believe blind scam artists, too? I've introduced you to a number of women over the years, and no one interests you. You know what, I think you haven't gotten over that vixen Yufen."

I chuckled and replied, "Maybe you're right," to appease her. I didn't feel like arguing about it.

"Do you want to go in and watch TV? Baoguo will be back soon."

I continued to stare at her blankly without speaking. Observing her hair, dyed black but still graying, I felt a sudden sense of grief and déjà-vu—for a second I could have sworn the woman standing before me was my mother. She seemed just as thin, and was shrinking as she aged. A cold draft blew through the kitchen; the old locust tree outside shook off a few gold leaves; I felt a stinging in my nose. I felt like . . . like standing up and hugging her.

"Do you . . . want to take a walk outside?" My sister became alarmed by my spaced out mental state.

I got up, went out alone, and sat down on the courtyard stoop to have a smoke.

The *hutong* was packed with parked cars, motor dollies, and those tricycles with metal cabins the handicapped use. My father's old workshop was long gone, replaced by an open-fire Peking duck restaurant. The old state-owned barber shop and the tailor shop run by a family from Zhejiang were also nowhere to be seen. Only the public toilet remained, still as foul as ever, though now its façade displayed a blue and white checkerboard pattern of ceramic tile. And of course no familiar faces passed down the lane.

Human memory really is unreliable. I could clearly remember this alley being long, wide, submerged in green shade or sprinkled with white locust flowers, and nowhere near as cramped and seedy as it looked that day. Street vendors used to lay their wares on blankets at the intersection on the east end. In the summers, the same group of old men sat with their straw hats, waving bamboo fans over their wrinkled stomachs as they eyed the emerald watermelons. In the winter, that corner was occupied either by a man from Shandong who cooked popcorn, or by others who sold caramel haw berries and cotton candy.

As I sat on the stoop and surveyed the cluttered street under the setting sun, I felt vaguely alienated from everything. Sacred fragments of my past life stirred my sluggish memory like echoes of a dying voice. I'm certainly not a nostalgic man; maybe my heart was heavy because this place used to be called "home." The scraping of tree branches against the roof; the moon in the leaves; the whirr of cicadas and the crash of rain; the smell of coal dust brushed from the furnace on an early morning—all used to accompany me to bed night after night and gently touch my soul in the darkness. But once that unique sort of loneliness settles in your chest, you feel afraid of time and life extinguished, as if your best years had been squandered completely.

Our place abutted the eastern end of the *hutong*; Jiang Songping lived on the western end. Our houses were separated by a private courtyard and a large compound for factory workers and their families. Residents rarely appeared in the clean little courtyard; on rare occasions you would see a black luxury sedan parked in front of the stone lion at its gate, and at night, a muted light would come on in one of the windows behind the courtyard trees and stay lit until morning. To this day I have no idea who lived there.

During our childhood, I often would watch Jiang Songping kick a filthy pig's bladder or push an iron hoop from the west end of the *hutong* to the east, turn just before the intersection, and go back. Our house sat right at the terminus of his mysterious, solitary route. Sometimes it wasn't a pig's bladder, iron hoop, or a slingshot he brought with him, but a date seed, which he'd drag along the wall as he walked. He scratched white line after white line on those dirty concrete walls, already scrawled with "FUCK" and "DESTROY," until he'd worn two little eyes and a mouth onto the pit's surface. No one paid any attention to him.

Every time he passed close by our door, my mother would peer surreptitiously out the window, sigh, and say that little shrimp from Pimply Jiang's household must be the loneliest kid she had ever seen. I never heard anybody say who Pimply Jiang was or what his family did for a living, nor did I ever meet him. It was like they never existed.

Jiang Songping eventually became friends with my sister and started playing games with the local girls. He turned out to be very good at all kinds of them—shuttlecock, jump rope, jacks. As for what moved him to hang out with girls, I expect it was loneliness.

I remember there was a spell when my sister was obsessed with playing jacks—not the modern metal ones, but the old ones made from sheep knuckles. She would take the S-shaped talus bones and polish them until they shone like jade, then dye them with red ink. She sewed her own neat little beanbags, filling them with expensive green mung beans—who knows how many times Ma slapped her for that. I never played the game myself, so I don't know much about the rules, but I've heard that you need at least four bones to play. Those weren't easy to get ahold of, back in those days. But somehow Jiang Songping possessed a magic pocket that could produce whatever my sister wanted. Whenever he presented the fruits of his labor to my sister, dropping the greasy black objects into her hand, she would laugh and ask, "Jiang Songping, do your parents own a butcher shop or something?"

For a period of time after the heart attack took my father away, I would go to his wireless repair shop almost every day. Somehow, sitting quietly at his workstation made me feel a little better. The other two repairmen in the shop pretended not to notice me; they neither engaged me, nor attended to what I did. Not even in the days immediately following my father's death did they ever offer a single word of comfort. My young heart couldn't handle such indifference, and retaliated with hate. I would stomp into the repair shop, sit down at my father's workstation, and stare at the half-repaired radio and the green screwdrivers. It was my privilege.

When it got dark, my mother would show up with tears

in her eyes and quietly take me home. That was how it went most days.

Until one day one of the repairmen, whom we called Horsewhip Xu, walked over and sat quietly with me for a long while. He smoked two cigarettes in a row, and then his expression became serious. He put a large hand on my shoulder, sighed heavily, and said, "I'll make you a deal, okay? If you can get that old semiconductor radio your father left behind to make noise again, you can take it home. How's that sound?"

At that age, having a radio of my very own was beyond my wildest dreams. So I started to play around with the dust-covered mess. Horsewhip Xu taught me some basic skills: how to re-coil tangled magnet wire evenly around a spool; how to scrape rust off the spring poles of a battery with a razor's edge; how to find a short circuit and reconnect it with a bead of hot solder; how to upgrade a system for a larger battery; how to install capacitors and resistors....

Two weeks or so later, my father's half-gutted radio finally made a sound. I still remember the first song I heard on it: the revolutionary opera *Night Assault on the White Tigers*, with Song Yuqing singing the lead.

If it could be said that I had an idol during those long years of my childhood, it would have been Song Yuqing. His presence, the way he carried himself, displayed a strength no Jay Chou or other such celebrity could even dream of imitating. Not even Wang Xiaogang, the movie heartthrob that Yufen's generation all fell in love with, could equal Song Yuqing's magnificence. To this day, the only Peking opera I ever learned was the part he sang from *Overthrow the American Imperialist Wolves*:

Debate has cleared our comrades' hearts and minds
To see beyond the enemies' evil scheme.
America's hunger for power knows no bounds;
To conquer the world is their undying dream.
When they fail, they hide the sword and talk of
     peace,
But soon, they wave their claws with avarice.

Listening to this song that sunny afternoon, I thought of my father and how great it would be if he were still alive, if he could listen to this music, if he could know that I learned how to fix a radio. As I fantasized, I started to cry. A gust of cold wind hit my face, my chest relaxed, and the stone that had been blocking my throat and pressing down on my heart suddenly disappeared.

I finally accepted the fact that my father was gone.

Horsewhip Xu sewed a black leather case for my radio. When my mother came to get me that evening, I heard him say to her, "This kid has talent, even more than Liankun (my father)."

"When he's older, you should take him as an apprentice," my mother replied.

"No, no." Horsewhip Xu put my radio into its case, snapped it shut, and placed it ceremoniously in my hands. "If he got into this business, what would we do for work?"

Hearing him say that tickled my mother. She held my hand as we walked home along the empty streets, our shoes squeaking in the fresh snow. My radio played an old army show tune, "The Old Landlord Checks the Barracks." At the start of our street, I caught sight of Jiang Songping standing in the darkness with a top in his hand, his mouth gaping in astonishment. He wore a leather cap with ear flaps, and his eyes opened wide. I can still remember the look of surprise mixed with envy apparent on his face.

The next morning, he promptly abandoned the gang of girls he'd been hanging out with and latched on to me. Our friendship began with him bugging me to borrow my radio.

In August of 1976, talk of earthquakes began swirling through the *hutong* alleys. Aftershocks from the later officially recognized July 28th Tangshan earthquake had shaken the boiler-room smokestack of the factory workers' compound off-center, its precipitous tilt alarming everyone who saw it and intensifying the fear in the hearts of local residents. An earthquake tent immediately appeared inside the compound, and soon everyone on Mahogany Street was making their own tent. Crude shelters multiplied among the trees next to the barbershop and on the open land along the old city moat. Some even made hammocks out of bedsheets and twine, stringing them up between two trees.

Terror quietly spread throughout the neighborhood.

The summer months of July and August are Beijing's rainiest season. One of the most surreal scenes I witnessed that year unfolded on a stormy night in mid-August. Under cover of darkness, my mother took my sister and me out to the old city moat to burn spirit money for my father. On the way home, we were suddenly caught in a torrential downpour. Midnight, the street completely empty, we got as far as the Sunward Photo Parlor when we discovered, right in the middle of the brick-lined road, an occupied, solitary army cot. On it lay a man well over six feet tall; he had wrapped himself up in plastic, and even held a propped-open umbrella in his hand. He slept, snoring loudly. Ma pointed at him and laughed, surprised that there were people in this world who feared death so much. Cui Lihua, whose teeth were chattering, chimed in, "You know, I think my brother's a little ... a little afraid too."

My mother often assured us that even if an earthquake knocked the house down, there weren't enough tiles left on our dilapidated roof to do us any harm. And besides, according to her, even if the damage were total and it flattened the whole city, it wouldn't be a big deal. Those people with government jobs and lots of money had something to live for, but the lives of people like us weren't really worth anything to begin with. If we died, we died. My sister and I found this ridiculous, and we resolved to address her pessimistic, confused thinking with barrage after barrage of complaints. Eventually, we drove her past her limit, and she hired someone to set up a small tent in the yard, with bunks made of stacked bricks. My sister and I slept in the tent, but my mother, determined as ever to tempt fate, continued to sleep in the house.

By then, Jiang Songping and I had become inseparable. His family lived on the fifth floor of an apartment building—earthquakes are no joke for those residents. It made perfect sense for him to ask to stay in our tent. My mother agreed to it without a second thought.

Although Jiang Songping was a solitary, pitiful-looking character, he was a natural politician. The things stuffed inside his head that he had seen and heard on his wanderings through the *hutongs* poured out spontaneously, making him quite likeable. He not only knew that Antonioni was posing as a movie director in order to infiltrate our country's borders and assassinate the Great Leader, Chairman Mao, he also knew that every pomegranate contained the same number of seeds: no matter how many different pomegranates you opened up, the number would always come to three hundred and sixty-five.

While he lived with us, my mother used to joke that he might as well just move in permanently and call her "Ma."

There was something else she used to say about him: "That kid is too smart. If there ever comes a day when capitalism really does return, I'm afraid the two of you will end up working for him."

We didn't pay attention to her; deep in our hearts, we were absolutely certain that, no matter what happened on this earth, capitalism would never return.

I never found out anything about Jiang Songping's parents or extended family—even the dangers of more earthquakes never drove them out into the open. I asked my mother if she knew anything, but she wouldn't say. She only quietly replied, "A horrible situation."

Even as terror spread out of control, it also filled us with irrepressible excitement. Schools closed; children with nothing to do ran around outside all day. Jiang Songping used to take me out past the city limits to go swimming in the river. We'd walk south from the east end of our alley, continue around a coal briquette factory and a Ming-dynasty walled outpost overgrown with weeds, then pass under a railway line to the river's edge. When we finished swimming, we'd lie in the peasants' watermelon fields, eat watermelon to our hearts' content, and take a nice, long nap. If we were hungry when we woke, there was always more watermelon.

When we were really bored, we'd sometimes go down to Horsewhip Xu's repair shop. The shop had hired a new repairman to take over my father's old workstation. It had also expanded its services, and now fixed tape recorders and black-and-white TVs, among other electronics. Horsewhip claimed that no man faced death as boldly as he did. He certainly wasn't about to waste his time messing with an earthquake tent! Cholera? US-Soviet nuclear war? Fatal earthquake? None of these things scared him. His outlook on life proved to be exactly the same as my mother's: "All men die only once. If somebody else dies, I can die, too. If they don't die, I might as well die anyway."

When the earthquake terror reached its zenith, and the old ladies from the local Residents Committee were patrolling the streets every day with their red bands tied to one arm, shouting through metal bullhorns at the locals to remind them that no matter what, they must not remove their socks before bed, Horsewhip Xu seemed to be the only man on Mahogany Street whose calm endured undisturbed. But Jiang Songping didn't believe any of it. He thought Horsewhip was deceiving everyone, and said to me, "You're crazy! Who doesn't fear death?! Horsewhip Xu looks like he doesn't care about an earthquake, like he's not afraid of anything. Have you seen that spring in the corner next to his desk, with an upside-down soda bottle on top? That's a homemade earthquake detector! If an earthquake hit, Horsewhip Xu would be the first one on the whole street to know. You don't believe me, let's do an experiment."

Jiang Songping pulled his slingshot out of his pocket and aimed through the window. He pulled the pink inner tube as far back as he could and released it. We heard a sharp *ting*, and the bottle toppled to the floor with a shattering crash.

Horsewhip Xu, who was immersed in the repair of a

broken radio, broke into a sudden fit of shivering, as if he'd been plugged into a socket. He looked confusedly around him, then bent down and inspected the broken glass on the floor. In a flash, he ripped off his old bifocals, threw them on the desk, and started to jump up and down, slapping his backside like a possessed man, and yelling, "Earthquake! Earthquake! Qiangui, Cabbage, let's go! Get out, you two, quick! Hurry, good God, it's an earthquake....!"

Jiang Songping dragged me under the windowsill, succumbing to a burst of laughter. "You fucking geezer! If it were an earthquake, you should be running your ass outside, not jumping around!" he sniggered with derision.

Of course, the myth of Horsewhip's fearlessness popped like a soap bubble. But I never laughed. I'm not sure why, but Songping's joke felt a little too cruel to me. I'm the kind of person who likes to let my perceptions float on the surface of things. I felt bad for Horsewhip, because even at that young age I had come to a personal realization: the best attributes of anyone or anything usually reside on the surface, which is where, in fact, all of us live out our lives. Everyone has an inner life, but it's best if we leave it alone. For as soon as you poke a hole through that paper window, most of what's inside simply won't stand up to scrutiny.

Even before the last ripples of the earthquake crisis had smoothed over, our lives had quietly changed. One day, Jiang Songping stopped showing up. He just vanished without giving me any explanation.

When I asked my mother, her face darkened and she snapped back, "What do you care? Someone like that.... I don't want you around him any more. Pretend he's dead. The quicker he dies, the quicker he'll be reborn!"

I went to find my sister. Her eyes were red and she looked

distracted. A long stretch of silence passed before she could say to me, sobbing, "Please don't say his name in front of me again, all right?"

Like I said, I'm not the kind of guy who likes digging for answers, so I stopped bothering them. I didn't know what had occurred between Jiang Songping and my sister, nor was I interested in knowing—it would only become another weight on my mind. Bumping into him on the street became awkward. Either he would sidestep quickly into the trees along the road, or he'd hug the wall, pretend not to see me, and keep on walking. I frequently felt like stopping him to ask what had happened. But in the end, I suppressed the squirming feeling in my chest. If I made up with him on my own, I felt like I'd be wronging my mother and sister. So I started to ignore him to save him from embarrassment.

As time passed, I gradually pushed his memory to the back of my mind.

In October of that year, I came home from school one day and walked straight into my sister's room. We both jumped. I could see that she had been sitting at the edge of her bed, counting pomegranate seeds in a porcelain basin. She reflexively put a hand over the mouth of the basin, then her face turned red and she pushed it aside, muttering, "Liar. What a liar!" Finally she stood up, tossed her braids, and stomped out.

Perhaps out of boredom, I picked up the bowl after she left and counted the seeds twice. It came out to three hundred and seventy-one both times. Six more seeds than Jiang Songping's eternal three hundred and sixty-five.

Four years later, in 1980, Jiang Songping and I started to hang out again. He had been taking remedial classes and was accepted into Beijing Communications College. After graduating from high school the year before, I had started to work at Red Capital Apparel to learn how to tailor. It turned out that his extended family really wasn't large at all: upon his acceptance into college, he held a banquet at Crane Garden Restaurant on Marco Polo Road to thank his previous teachers, and only his aunt showed up. Riding my bike home through Dashilar Market after work one day, I randomly bumped into him. Neither of us knew what to say. Perhaps this awkwardness prompted Jiang Songping to ask if I wanted to come to the banquet.

I couldn't think of any way to refuse, so I accepted.

As I didn't have anything to bring to the celebration, I spent the following three weeks in Horsewhip Xu's workshop building him a shortwave radio. By then, Horsewhip Xu, paralyzed from a stroke, lay on a ratty old sofa for most of the day. Still, he didn't forget to remind me gently that it was illegal to listen to Deng Lijun or Voice of America on the radio.

Later on, Songping told me he had immediately thrown my gift into a runoff ditch by his school without ever listening to it once. Apparently, it brought back his nightmare from years ago, back in the earthquake tent. He said it would be impossible for him to forget what had happened, unless he went insane. Already, after so many years, his struggle with that memory had utterly exhausted him. He asked me not to be offended—he had no choice. It turned out that mysterious occurrence was even more serious than I had imagined. Not only did it weigh on his conscience, it remained an obstacle in our friendship. Every once in a while, he would cast a searching gaze toward me and the shadow of the unspeakable event would rise up and smother us both.

Jiang Songping majored in telecommunications. In order to keep our friendship on equal footing, I signed up for classes at Red Flag Night College without telling my family. Red Flag Night College didn't have a telecommunications major, so I picked Marxist Economics at random. Out of ten classes, the only one I could barely tolerate was College Language Arts. I sweated it out for over a year, then gave up.

In his junior year Songping contracted hepatitis; the school put him in quarantine at the Temple of the Earth Hospital. I visited him every weekend, spending whole afternoons with him sitting in that gloomy corridor. One day before I left, I finally mustered the courage to say something I had been meaning to say for many years: "No matter what happened back then between you and my sister, no matter how awful or filthy it might have been, I would forgive you completely. It's been ancient history for years now, so can you please just forget about it? Like...like it never existed. Okay?"

Songping must not have expected that I would strike right at his soft spot. His face, turned a waxy yellow from both hepatitis and stress, glowed faintly pink. He stared at me in shock for a long while. Then he leaped up, grabbed my wrist, and with his thick lips quivering and tears in his eyes, said, "Brother, what the hell kind of good does it do for you to forgive me? I can't even forgive myself!"

My sister cooked dumplings for us that night, and Chang Baoguo and I got sloshed. My sister's face, ravaged by time and covered with warts and liver spots, still retained enough composure to hide a measure of sunlit past along with a dark secret from her youth.

My brother-in-law toasted me again and again, slapping me unnecessarily on the shoulder. His unnatural affection made me nervous. He said that if it hadn't been for the accident in Changping, if it hadn't left him crippled and unable to look for work ever again, he'd never have been forced into such a hard decision as asking me to move. Then he said something that startled me: "Shit, society today even forces family members to go for each other's throats."

I recalled Jiang Songping's warning from a few days ago. Though I knew it wouldn't matter either way, I couldn't help peeking under the table. My brother-in-law wore a pair of beaten-up old walking shoes.

As we got drunker, I let the impulse to reciprocate my brother-in-law's earnestness get the best of me, and swore that I would immediately move out. I felt a profound regret the instant the words left my mouth, as if I actually had another place to go to after moving out of their hole-cursed home. I would never have thought that even Jiang Songping's factory would be closed to me.

Throughout the evening, my sister interrupted our banter with her words of counsel, annoying me to no end. She repeatedly pushed me to meet this lisping co-worker of hers. How did she put it? That if I never got married and had a family, if I ended up floating through the world like a wandering ghost, I wouldn't only be ignoring our mother's last words, but father's spirit would somehow know and he'd never find any peace. She went on and on, unable to control herself, and soon the waterworks erupted.

In my half-inebriated condition, I agreed to a date. We

settled on next Saturday. A venomous flame instantly consumed my heart, spreading an incredible feeling of self-loathing.

Quietly I accelerated the pace of my drinking in order to pass out sooner.

5. ROAD TO HEAVEN

IF YOU live in Beijing and like fine teas, you've no doubt heard about Malian Avenue. It's not far from our place on Mahogany Street, in the south part of the city just outside of Guang'an Gate in the Xuanwu District. When I was little, that area was still considered the suburbs; my sister and I used to sneak into the orchards there to steal apricots. Now it's the largest tea market in Beijing, the sidewalks packed with one-room storefronts run by tea sellers from Fujian and Zhejiang.

The woman my sister set me up with, Hou Meizhu, lived in Little Red Temple, a neighborhood right next to Malian Avenue.

That Saturday afternoon, I drove to the house to pick up my sister, then the two of us headed over to Little Red Temple to meet her.

Whenever you're set up on a blind date, you inevitably try to picture what she looks like based on her name. Everybody does it. *Mei-zhu*, or "beautiful pearl"—you can imagine how eagerly I looked forward to meeting her. You can also imagine how much sharper the disappointment felt when faced with the actual person.

Dinner took place at a Wild Swans Dumpling House on the second floor of a second-rate supermarket. The restaurant was greasy and loud; making conversation required that we raise our voices and practically yell at each other across the table. This quickly became not only awkward but unsettling.

As far as looks go, while I wouldn't go so far as to call her unattractive, she was still a ways off from the "pretty and well-proportioned" Lihua had promised. Her short hair parted in the middle made her seem younger, perhaps, but her square face made her look almost androgynous. If you saw her on the street, you couldn't be sure of her gender at first glance. My sister constantly warned me not to expect every woman in creation to be dangerously sexy like Yufen. I guess I just preferred Yufen's type. Plus the sharp smell of cheap perfume turned me off.

Still, the very moment I met Meizhu I could see she was an upstanding, compassionate person. Even if I didn't want to date her, it wouldn't be right to deliberately offend her. She had brought along her eighth-grade son. The boy, who had a head as round as a basketball, clearly realized that this situation could affect him in some way. He wasn't very friendly to me, which was understandable. Hunched over his game console, he peered up at me every now and then with a hostile glint in his eyes.

My sister, seeing my lack of interest, kept signaling Meizhu to be more engaging with looks and tugs on her sleeve. Lihua didn't really know how to deal with the unfolding disaster, so she kept repeating the same sentence, which caused my insides to squirm: "Well, we'll all be family soon enough."

The more she said it, the more anxious I grew. I could tell it was making Hou Meizhu uncomfortable, too. But she couldn't stand up to my sister's pushiness the way I could, and so with a perfunctory smile she picked up a dumpling with her chopsticks and dropped it into my bowl. This seemingly inconsequential gesture touched me in an astonishing way—no one besides my mother had ever helped me to food like that. My heart warmed half a degree; I actually started to consider what it would be like to marry her.

Once my sister saw evidence of emotional activity on Hou Meizhu's part, she turned to face me. "The two of you can talk about music. You know, what a coincidence, Meizhu is also a what-do-you-call-it you're always talking about—an audiologist. So the two of you have plenty to talk about."

By then, I had already established a bottom line: "Anything is possible in this universe except for you marrying her," and I was feeling much calmer. Out of politeness (and, of course, out of curiosity about what my sister considered an "audiologist") I asked Meizhu what kind of music she listened to and what type of sound system she owned. Meizhu's face turned red. She spoke with an impediment, as if she had a piece of candy in her mouth. She said she liked buying tapes and CDs to listen to in her free time, but that her son had broken her sound system a couple days ago, so now sometimes it worked, sometimes not.

"That's no problem. He'll fix it for you. Once we're done eating, he can take a look at it. I guarantee he'll fix it for you in minutes. Meizhu's a really good singer," my sister laughed, turning to me. "I mean seriously good. Every year when we have our New Year's party at the office, she always sings 'Road to Heaven,' and it's just as good as Han Hong's rendition."

My sister gave Meizhu a poke in the arm and whispered something to her, as if she were trying to persuade her to sing a line. Of course Meizhu shook her head and waved a hand. Strangely enough, while she resisted, she kept her timid gaze locked on mine, as if holding out for my reaction. I returned her the most severe look I could manage, pleading and begging her to do the right thing and not sing. For someone to break out in song in a filthy, noisy little dumpling restaurant like this one would be too much to bear. To make Lihua forget her stupid idea as soon as possible, I turned to address the boy sitting next to me.

In a polite tone I asked his name, where he went to school, and so on. He paid absolutely no attention to my low-voiced questioning, not even bothering to look up.

"An adult asked you a question. You mustn't be impolite," Meizhu admonished her son.

The boy finally raised his head and looked me over once more with a vicious glitter in his eyes. "Can you answer me a question first?" he sneered.

"Of course!" I spoke without thinking.

"Can the phrase 'fresh as summer flowers' be used to describe a boy?"

"That's hard to say." The question had caught me off guard. I had no idea how to reply, so I gave a conciliatory smile and added, "But I expect so!"

"Wrong!" the boy shouted back. It seemed he had weighed me, found me wanting, and moved on. He returned to his video game.

I remembered that I had to get up early the next day to take my visiting cousin to see Tanzhe Temple, so I stuck it out until the end of dinner, then immediately stood up and excused myself. Meizhu didn't object, but my sister wouldn't have it; she was determined to send me over to Meizhu's place to "get acquainted." Hearing Lihua's tone of voice you'd think I had already agreed to marry her, or something. She mentioned the broken sound system (just waiting to be fixed!) to make it harder for me to back out respectfully. Now, I admit I can be pretty thick when it comes to personal relationships, but I could easily catch the drift behind Lihua's forceful behavior. And that realization made me very uncomfortable.

Seven or eight minutes later, as we turned down a smoggy back alley, I looked behind me to discover that my sister, who had been keeping a few steps behind us, was suddenly nowhere to be seen. Her amateur disappearing act didn't surprise Meizhu, nor me for that matter.

Meizhu lived in a tiny one-and-a-half-room apartment. The front door opened into the bathroom; a narrow hallway, barely wide enough for a small fold-out table, served as both dining and sitting room. This lead to a similarly cramped kitchen, with strings of dried sausages and garlic hanging on the walls, making the room look even messier and more chaotic. Farther along a particle-board screen split another room in half, with a small bed on one side and a desk and simple bookshelf on the other—presumably the boy's living quarters. Meizhu's bedroom was located at the end of the hall. As soon as her son walked into the house, he ran into her room to watch television, slamming the door so hard it made the calendar that hung by the front door swing back and forth.

Her so-called "sound system" was covered with a square of brown silk and sat on a low shelf next to her refrigerator. I didn't know whether to laugh or to cry when I saw it: a dual-deck tape recorder with a CD console and nothing more. Calling it a child's English practice machine might have been closer to the mark. I pressed a round button and the cover of the CD deck popped up with a stiff *snap* that startled me. Using my cigarette lighter as a torch, I peered inside and found the problem fairly quickly: the LED reader on the bottom needed adjusting. Meizhu emptied every drawer in her house looking for a Phillips head screwdriver but couldn't find one. So I made do with a fruit knife and a pair of tweezers, eventually fixing her "sound system."

I had also polished the LED lens after moving it, so it wasn't improbable that the sound quality had improved. But for her to flatter me by saying it sounded better than the day she bought the stereo seemed a bit of a stretch. She put on Han Hong's recording of "Road to Heaven" and sang along, casting a pitiable glance my way as it ended, as if begging to be encouraged to sing it again. Naturally, I paid no attention. Funny, though: when she sang, her pronunciation became impeccable, with no trace of that garbled sound like she had something in her mouth. I couldn't help but feel quietly impressed. As she prepared to play it over again, I stood up to announce that I should be going.

She hesitated for a second, then reminded me in her mumbling voice; "But, you had a drink at dinner...."

"I had a little; why?" I looked straight at her, not entirely sure what she was insinuating.

"Well, if you leave now, what would happen if you ran into the police?"

"I only had one beer. Even if they did test me it wouldn't register."

"Don't be foolish. It's always better to be careful. Stay for a while. I just made some tea; have a cup first and sober up a little before you go." Meizhu turned off her CD player and ushered me over to the table in the sitting room.

Meizhu had laid out a special tea set, with a delicate terra-cotta pot and four miniature glazed cups. She said she had bought them in Yixing, when she and her ex-husband had traveled to Hangzhou for their honeymoon. She was using them now for the first time after all those years. She blushed as she said this, probably with regret. Bringing up her former husband in a situation like this didn't really seem appropriate. I took a few mouthfuls of tea: bitter, sharp chrysanthemum with a pungent mildew taste. I wanted to remind her that ordinary chrysanthemum tea didn't require a fancy set like this one. Also that being relatively poor wasn't something to be embarrassed about; being poor and parroting the habits of the rich, however, was embarrassing. But when I saw her pop a couple pills with her tea (she could have been discreet but chose not to be), I changed my mind and asked her if she was feeling okay.

Meizhu told me that seven or eight years ago she was diagnosed with thyroid cancer. She had surgery, everything's fine now, nothing to worry about, thyroid cancer being one of the least dangerous kinds of cancer and easy to cure. The pills merely ensured the effectiveness of the treatment....

"And did my sister know about your situation?"

"What thichuation?"

"The thichuation with the canther." I realized that I had unintentionally imitated her speech impediment. Luckily, she didn't seem to take offense.

"Of course she knew. She was the one who took me to the hospital."

Meizhu must not have noticed the fury rising in my face. She went on to say that she had heard someone was forcing me out of my house, and that I had nowhere to go. If I liked, she said, I could stay with her and her son—the marriage license could be worked out later.

My fury, as you can imagine, reached a peak. I nearly

shouted as I informed Meizhu that the person forcing me out was none other than my own sister, Cui Lihua!

I chatted with Meizhu until late in the evening. To be honest, I felt extremely well-disposed toward the woman. Lisp or no lisp, she was a compassionate, honest person, no doubt. In a world like ours, individuals like her are scarce and becoming harder and harder to find. That her situation was so much more desperate than mine triggered a sort of impulse within me—the naïve impulse to care for her for the rest of her life. Yet this idea only flickered once, then disappeared. As I cast an eye over the cluttered, airless apartment, I realized with some distress that even if I did marry her, where the hell would I put all my sound equipment?

I made my way home to Shijingshan and went straight to bed, but couldn't fall asleep. A late autumn draft filtered through the crack in the wall, filling the room with a crisp chill. Frail mosquitoes poured in, probably wanting to escape the deathly cold outside; they whined sluggishly above my head. The mosquitoes weren't the ones keeping me awake: something Songping recently said to me echoed in my head. His mother, who had run off to Sha'anxi province and remarried while he was still a child, had suddenly sent word that she would be moving back to Beijing to stay with him. Familial love, Songping told me, was basically just a thin sheet of ice floating on open water. As long as you didn't poke it with a stick or throw a stone on it, it would stay unbroken. But as soon as you put a foot down to test its strength, it would shatter.

My sister knew perfectly well I had nowhere to move to. In order to get me out of her apartment as fast as possible, she shut her eyes and pushed me onto Hou Meizhu, with her lisp and her even more difficult life. She had withheld a detail as significant as Meizhu's cancer from me. I was be-ginning to feel that Lihua wasn't as good a person as I had been willing to believe. The crying over the phone must have been fake—all that about Chang Baoguo kicking her in her groin, pissing blood or whatever—of course it all had been bullshit! She only harbored one purpose, which was to get me the fuck out as soon as she could. I should have seen it long before: her letting me live in this apartment wasn't an act of kindness. After our mother died, half of the courtyard on Mahogany Street should have been mine. How could I have not noticed that after marrying Chang Baoguo, that scheming bastard, her behavior, her tone of voice, her morals, even her appearance had been gradually changing to resemble his.

I woke up at 1:15, smoked a cigarette, then at 3:40, smoked another, until finally nodding off just before sun-rise, instantly slipping into a dream.

I dreamt I saw my mother, seated in the lotus pose on an iridescent cloud, floating toward me from far away. She looked stately in a black jacket with a silk front and an up-right collar—the burial clothes my sister had bought for her. Her face was as white as plaster, expressionless. Even though I knew it was only a dream, and that it was my mother I dreamt about, I still felt afraid.

With sincerity, I asked her if I should marry Hou Meizhu. She didn't smile. She gave a silent but definite shake of the head, then vanished from sight.

The following morning, I took my cousin out for a tour of Tanzhe Temple. I could hardly believe that I dreamt such a dream. Perhaps, without knowing it, I had already resolved not to marry Meizhu, and my mother's appearance served as one more excuse to avoid my own responsibilities.

6. AUTOGRAPH

In MID-November, my cousin and his daughter came up from Yancheng to visit Beijing. My apartment wasn't far from the scenic area at Mentougou, so my sister asked if I could take them out for a day—to Jietai Temple, Tanzhe Temple, anywhere would be fine. After my date with Meizhu, my loathing for Cui Lihua and her husband reached a new high, and yet while we were on our excursion, I reminded myself repeatedly to not let my anger out on my innocent cousin and his child.

On the way home that evening, I took the two of them to dinner at a farmhouse restaurant. While looking for the bathroom outside, I caught sight of a "For Sale" sign pasted onto a brick wall of the courtyard. The space for sale turned out to be two large, square rooms that bordered the western wall of the courtyard. An old locust tree with a magpie nest in its branches stood outside the front door; two big pumpkins grew on the rooftop, their dry vines scraping and rustling in the autumn breeze. I found the owner. He said the asking price was three hundred and eighty thousand yuan, which seemed a little ridiculous to me. Still, it was only a half-hour drive from my apartment in Shijingshan. I made a mental note.

The next morning, after sending off my cousin and his daughter, I returned to the property. The owner quickly agreed to lower the price to three hundred and fifty thousand. He cautioned that the house only came with a forty-year purchase lease, no seventy-year available. I didn't have a problem with that. Forty years seemed like more than enough time to me—I couldn't imagine living that long anyway.

The interior of the house was in good shape, the spacious courtyard a real luxury. As the rooms faced east and a creek ran behind the property, I could imagine the summer sun heating the place up, and plenty of mosquitoes. The owner promised to include a plot of land in the courtyard as part of the deal, so that I could grow "totally pollution-free vegetables." If I didn't garden, his wife could garden for me. She had a quick tongue, a light step, and a glow to her cheeks so bright it looked like she had rouged them. I hadn't come across anyone so healthy and energetic as her in a long time. I asked them when I could move in if I decided to buy. "Any time," they replied. Apparently, they needed the money. Their profligate son, a student at the University of Aix-Marseille II, continued to flush away all the money the old couple had managed to save through years of frugal living. With voices full of regret, they confessed that they had no choice but to sell the family house. Still, they didn't forget to remind me twice that Marseille, located in the south of France, was the setting for *The Count of Monte Cristo.*

The house became a fantasy that ensnared me. For several successive nights I dreamt of the courtyard and the magpie nest in the old locust tree. In one such dream, I watched Yufen work in the garden while reclining on a deck chair in the shade of the tree. To my astonishment, she paused from her weeding to hitch up her dress and squat down among the cucumber leaves and trellised morning glories to pee. The afternoon sun made the air as hot as an oven; all was silent save the hurried, spattering stream of her urine driving a shallow hole in the garden soil. I tried to lower my head to peek under her dress and banged my forehead on the bedside. As I woke, the image of Yufen's bewitching smile still glowed in the darkness before my blurry eyes; then it faded, swept away by a cold breeze.

I decided to buy the house. I hoped that once I fulfilled this desire, all my other problems would disappear into thin air.

A stupid plan slowly began to emerge in my mind.

You might remember how, a couple weeks back in his study, Songping had recommended to me a client named Ding Caichen, who wanted me to build him "the best sound system in the world." I have no idea what would really qualify as the "best." If it's just about the price, and you simply want the most expensive stereo system in the world, you can spend tens of millions without much trouble. Still, based on my own biased opinion (as well as on my financial limitations), the Autograph line of speakers from Tannoy are the best you'll ever experience.

In fact, I happened to have a pair of them babies myself.

In the 1990s, Mou Qishan, the celebrity tycoon, was a household name in Beijing. He liked calligraphy, climbing mountains, and hanging out with female movie stars—all an open secret. Other rumors, however, told of his eccentric, often unpredictable, behavior. The wildest story I heard was that he could show up at any event unseen because he wore an invisibility cloak. I never witnessed this myself, so I don't know the real story behind it. But Mou Qishan presided as a godfather figure in the hi-fi community. Every year during the Lantern Festival he'd rent out an entire floor of the Powealth Mall and set up a private exhibition of high-end audio equipment for only us professionals. Then he'd take us all for hot pot to chat about our current business. He loved Bartók and Prokofiev—clearly no mere layman's tastes. I met him myself at two such dinners, which ought to dispel the invisibility cloak rumor.

In August of 1999, while climbing the summit of Mount Minya Konka in Tibet, Mou Qishan got caught in an avalanche. The news hit us pretty hard. I even attended a small memorial service for him, organized by the community. Bartók's "Evening in the Village" played on repeat during the service.

After Mou Qishan died, his wife organized a semi-public auction of certain items from his estate to pay off his debts. I say "semi-public" because not many people actually knew about it. Jiang Songping had the runs that day, and couldn't even leave the house. He called me up, asking me to go try my luck and possibly find him a bargain among that bounty of beautiful equipment.

During the auction, all eyes remained fixed on Mou Qishan's scrolls of calligraphy and paintings, his antiques and rosewood furniture. No one paid any attention to the pair of hexagonal Autograph speakers that stood bashfully in a corner like gorgeous twin sisters. From the time I entered the building to the end of the auction, my eyes never left them, not even for a second. I guarded them silently, not daring to breathe too loudly until the auction floor emptied. By the time I had acquired the speakers for a mere eighty thousand yuan, I felt totally drained, as if I had been drunk the whole time, the world around me shimmering like a mirage.

The Autograph line first appeared in 1954. They're considered the magnum opus of the great engineer Guy R.

Fountain—supposedly designed to maximize the potential of the 15-inch Dual Concentric speaker drive. Having selected the best horn driver, Fountain went on to create an incredibly complex, almost labyrinthine amplification path for the sound. Of course, the English word "autograph" has plenty of direct equivalents in Chinese, but for whatever reason, someone in the hi-fi community translated it as "autobiography," and the mistake has been accepted as the norm. Original production of the Autograph stopped in 1974, due to the exorbitant production costs and the increasing scarcity of samarium cobalt, a rare earth magnet used in the driver. The speakers have become valuable collector's items. To my knowledge, there are only three sets in the whole of East Asia. The ones you now see in the second-hand markets are either copies or Autograph minis.

After buying the speakers, a fear that they would suddenly disappear kept me from telling Jiang Songping. Nor did I ever reveal their real value to Yufen. One day I came home from a delivery to find Yufen cleaning the speaker boxes with a goddamn steel wool scrubber and White Cat disinfectant. She scrubbed hard to make them "look a little newer," and even put a huge fucking flowerpot on top of each box. I almost fainted.

At the time of our divorce, I only demanded one thing: that she leave me all the audio equipment, including the Autograph speakers. That should tell you much I loved them. My sister could only shake her head and call me an idiot. That bastard Chang Baoguo proved even cruder. One Lantern Festival, the two of them visited me at Shijingshan. After a couple of drinks, Chang Baoguo started to lecture me. He said that the primary cause of our divorce could be traced to Yufen's infidelity. If that filthy bitch couldn't keep her legs together and wanted other guys on the side, then from a legal standpoint she should be entitled to nothing. Only an idiot would agree to give her the apartment. After bearing this for a good while, I eventually had enough. I walked into the kitchen, grabbed the cleaver and tossed it onto the dining room table. I warned him that if he said another word about Yufen, either I'd kill him or he could kill me.

Chang Baoguo called me "chicken shit" a few times, then grabbed his wife and stomped off without finishing dinner.

In truth, giving the apartment to Yufen in no way turned out to be a bad deal for me. I had gone over the calculation a thousand times. Our place in Shangdi East cost less than a hundred and eighty thousand yuan. By the time of our divorce, the Autograph set was worth two hundred thousand or more on the second-hand market. Seems like an equitable division of assets to me. Plus, the building being so close to Yufen's workplace made it perfectly reasonable for her to want to stay and keep her easy commute. Then those memories of how poor we had been through our years together, her staying by my side as we barely scraped by, were embarrassing for me to recall. Even that three-thousand-yuan jade pendant she had always pined for hovered beyond my reach.

To keep the speakers in good working order and prevent the sound from deteriorating into fuzziness, I warmed them up once every two weeks or so, usually during the quiet hours of the night. I'd pull out a recording of an Italian string quartet's rendition of Mozart (my favorite composer to this day), or Walter Gieseking playing Ravel or Debussy, and listen to it at a low volume for a couple hours.

I knew that the technical specs of my own system kept the speakers from producing their best sound. But it was like seeing a young, beautiful woman right after she wakes in the morning, face fresh and unwashed, free of make-up. It felt more than enough. I could sense her understated elegance, her every gesture, her intoxicating allure.

Sometimes, when the familiar music separated from the darkness to dance in the living room with its cracked wall, my breath would catch in my throat and hot tears crowd my eyes. It felt as if Yufen had never left me, as if her radiant face emerged out of the music. It felt as if I had no business enjoying this luxury in such a polluted, chaotic world.

No matter where I ended up, or what bitterness, loneliness, or humiliation I had to swallow, I only needed to think of those Autograph speakers, standing silent against the living room wall, waiting for me to come home, and I would hear an assuring voice in my ear: "Your life isn't so bad, my friend—a little hope waits around the corner."

You can probably guess the gist of my stupid plan by now. That's correct: I would sell my Autograph speakers to Ding Caichen.

No choice, no way out of it, it had to be done.

I thought back to that day many years ago when I paraded Yufen in front of my family, and of the surprise, hesitation, and worry that crossed my mother's face. "Marrying this woman for somebody else." Those were her words. She even had a smile on her face when she said it—a smile that betrayed an almost imperceptible, vaguely terrifying mystery.

It was past one in the morning by the time I got back from sending Yufen home that night. Ma's congestion seemed worse; she sat on a stool in the yard, wheezing heavily. Lihua pulled me to one side and gravely asked if we should take her to the hospital. I didn't want to consider that at the moment. I brushed her off and marched directly up to my mother. I pulled her up from the stool and demanded evidence for whatever she meant about Yufen.

Moonlight turned her face a soft, pale blue. She sighed faintly and said, "Sometimes poor people get lucky enough to find treasures, too. But you'll never be able to keep her. You won't like to hear this, but the most you can do with a woman like this is take your turn and enjoy it. When the time comes, she'll still have to go where she must go."

She noticed my dumbfounded expression and stroked my arm, saying, "Child, that you even get a turn at all is because of good karma passed down from our ancestors. Tell me, what's the most valuable thing anyone can ever have? It's your life, isn't it? But you can hold on to it as tightly as you can for every waking hour, and you'll still have to let it go when the time comes, won't you?"

I'll be honest. For a long time after that, I quietly ridiculed her, hated her, to the point of hoping she would die a little sooner. And when she finally passed away, I didn't shed a single tear for her at the funeral. It was as if she had held on to life for four more years after being diagnosed with a terminal disease just to see her ill-willed prophecy come true.

But then, right as I was about to go through with it and sell my Autograph speakers, I suddenly understood everything.

And I began to see my mother as the wisest woman in the world, and I loved her more dearly than I did myself.

But enough of that for the moment. Having decided to sell the Autograph set to Ding Caichen as part of "the greatest sound system in the world," my main consideration involved finding and building a stereo system that would be worthy of it. Imagine a father sending his favorite daughter off to be married; no matter how unwilling he is to let go, he must steel himself and collect her dowry. At the very least, he has to find her a nice enough dress to send her off looking fabulous.

The first question to solve was the amplifier. The KT88 had plenty of good, hard push to it, but I found the sound too rigid, and too brittle at higher frequencies. By comparison, the EL34 produced a much more delicate sound, though the density of amplification never seemed sufficient and the sound lacked flavor. I thought about installing a 300B. As everyone knows, the sound produced by the 300B is beyond comparison. Sadly, however, the output maxed out at twelve watts, and I couldn't guarantee that would be enough to satisfy my beloved Autographs. I could connect two amplifiers together as a "push-pull" set, which would double the wattage, but artificially increasing the output wouldn't be much different than giving a man with erectile dysfunction an overdose of Viagra. After a long period of indecision, I decided to take a bigger risk: I'd assemble her with a single 845.

The 845 tube amplifier is known by hi-fi experts as "The King." It would work perfectly with the direct-heading RCA cathode ray tube (which has its own nickname, "The

Pillar of Heaven") I had been saving for so long. Still, building a high-performance 845 was no easy task for an at-home technician like myself. Working with such high voltage requirements involved a certain measure of risk. I had attempted it twice in the past. The first time I got lucky and everything came out right; the second time a misrouted current fried the skin on my palms and I had to stop. But to give my darling Autographs what they wanted, I decided to step into the fray once more.

Thank heaven the process went smoothly. An HR director from Lenovo somehow got wind of my activities and came over to listen to the amplifier. He proceeded to waste the whole evening trying to convince me to sell it to him instead. I refused him.

Concerning the question of the audio source, I was deadlocked between the Swiss Studer 730 and the English Linn 12. I preferred the 730—tracking this rare item down on the Chinese market, however, would be nearly impossible, and ordering one from abroad through eBay would be more trouble than it was worth. The Linn 12—or Lotus 12, as professionals called it, the word "linn" sounding so much like *lian* for "lotus"—was widely recognized by the hi-fi community as the best CD player out there, with a sound quality that closely approximated vinyl. I had found a used one for sale online, the seller located in Tongzhou, which bordered the southwest corner of the city. He wanted eighty thousand for the 24-bit unit. I could vaguely recall that the ad had been posted for three months straight without any bids; buyers probably thought the price too high for a secondhand unit. I figured I could maybe gouge him a tiny bit, get the price down to seventy. So I rang him up, and we haggled for a spell. The final price we agreed on:

sixty-eight thousand. After hanging up, I picked up pen and paper to make some simple calculations.

Tannoy Autograph speakers were a hot commodity in hi-fi markets everywhere in the world, usually selling the minute they hit the floor. One set the same size as mine sold recently in Melbourne for forty-five thousand dollars, or nearly three hundred thousand yuan. So to offer mine to Ding Caichen for two hundred and fifty was a bargain. For the 845 amplifier I would only charge him forty thousand; for Vovox monitor signal cables and microphone cables, thirty-five thousand; then the Linn 12 would be sixty-eight thousand on top of everything else. (As you must have guessed, I had yet to buy this machine. Doing so would use up almost all my savings, but I had already decided to resell it to Ding Caichen for the same price.) The overall cost for the system soared above three hundred and ninety thousand yuan. This would give me enough money to buy the courtyard outright, with a little extra cash left over. Thus, while I would be weighed down with the sadness of relinquishing something I loved, wouldn't this sensible decision bring security and relief?

I rang Ding Caichen. An automated recording informed me that he was temporarily unable to take my call. So I left my name and number, hung up, and suffered a tortuous wait. Fortunately, after only twenty minutes, Ding Caichen called me back.

His voice sounded gentle and frail, though perfectly clear. I introduced myself, mentioning my connection with Jiang Songping. Then I told him about the sound system I could build for him, listing the components, capabilities, estimated time of delivery. He listened to me with patience, offering an occasional one-word response to anything I said: "Good."

I should note that during our phone conversation, I didn't pick up anything unusual about him, let alone any trace of the dangerous mystique that Jiang Songping had described. He seemed like a perfect gentleman, at least from his voice. Twice he asked if I could speak a little slower because of his poor reception. As I gushed on and on about the ethereal auditory experience the system would provide for him, he even chuckled and commented, "Oh, really?"

If anything could be interpreted as suspicious during our conversation, I guess it could be that, well, his mind didn't seem fully present. His responses came slow and slightly delayed, as if he had just woken up. And then I did hear him make these weird noises while we spoke. When I told him that the overall price for the system would run around three hundred ninety thousand yuan, and asked if he'd be willing to pay a portion in advance, he immediately responded: "Not a problem. Here, why don't you give me an account number and I'll wire a third—will a third work? a hundred and thirty thousand—directly to you. Will that be acceptable?"

I gave him my ICBC account number. To confirm, I requested that he repeat the numbers back to me. Again the mumbling noises, followed by, "I'm sorry...I'm actually sitting on the toilet right now, so I can't write anything down. Must be food poisoning, upset stomach. How about this: just text the number to me and I'll have someone wire the cash to you."

So I texted him my account number, then sent another text asking him to confirm receipt. The reason for my circumspection should be clear: this would be, after all, the biggest job I had ever taken on in all my years in this business—I had to make sure everything went smoothly. But

Ding Caichen's reply text came with an unpleasant surprise:

> Hufang Bridge West, Unit 37 Apt A. Try to
> be perfect and where's the fun, eh? Green
> light. Bring a few extra hands with you,
> this might be our last opportunity.

Obviously a wrong number. Ding Caichen must have made an error and accidentally sent me a text meant for someone else—a common enough mistake, nothing strange about it. Yet, as I turned it over in my head, the content of the message caused my suspicions about this new client to deepen. I noted before that I've never had any interest in other people's private lives, no burning desire to get to the bottom of anything. I could easily have sent Ding Caichen a message telling him that he'd sent his text to the wrong person, but for some reason I couldn't calm my pounding heart. My intuition—that sense of foreboding that always ended up coming true—restrained me from texting back. You're probably aware of the kind of trouble that can come from accidentally learning someone else's secrets in today's society.

Fortunately, Ding Caichen's confirmation arrived five minutes later:

> Received, not to worry.

Sixteen days later, on my seventeenth trip to the ATM in the post office below my apartment, I saw that Ding Caichen's hundred and thirty thousand had posted to my account. I relaxed, feeling ashamed of my own paranoia and of the two-plus weeks of insomnia and wild delusions. I always imagine the worst, even when I have no cause to.

Over-cautiousness clearly becomes a bad habit that needs to be fixed.

7. THE LOTUS 12

EVER SINCE I first fell in love with the hi-fi industry I've been buying equipment from audiophiles across the world. For every purchase, anything from speaker boxes, antique Victrola horns, amplifiers, or CD players, to resistors, capacitors, or record needles, the seller and I have always followed an unwritten rule: "Money comes in, goods go out." I've sent money to unfamiliar accounts everywhere, from Hong Kong, which has a relatively good reputation, to shadier places like Henan, and I've never had a problem. Not only have I never been swindled, instances of hidden defects or poor-quality replacements have been extraordinarily rare. In an age where scams and cons are so common you can't keep up with their manifestations, you have to admit that for the second-hand hi-fi industry to maintain such a standard of trust is a miracle. It also explains why I stick around and continue to love my job, even as the client pool grows shallower and my profits thinner. No doubt, our community is still a haven. I personally attribute this to a higher-than-average ethical conscience among members of the community, shaped by the influence of classical music on human character. You can plainly observe: in an age where brutal competition has pitted friends and neighbors against each other, classical music has served as a special medium to bring like-minded people together into a close-

knit community, out of which an honest business environment has naturally formed. If you wanted to call it a
"collective," or even a "utopia," I wouldn't object. At any
rate, for many years I've felt proud to be a part of it.

Yet my optimism once encountered the ridicule of one
of my clients, a lawyer named Bai Cheng'en. Counsel Bai
was one of my steadier clients. His musical tastes tended
toward the Renaissance and the Baroque periods, and he
only listened to vinyl. A few years back, he received his law
degree at The Hague, then set up a private practice in Beijing's central business district specializing in international
cases. He harbored a deep-seated contempt for the poor
that used to make me very uncomfortable—for instance,
he never took a case for less than a two-hundred-thousand-
yuan retainer. But to be fair, once I got to know him, I
quickly realized that he was among the few in our society
with the gift of real insight. Every time I talked to him, I
would always leave feeling as if my eyes had just been opened.

One afternoon, he listened with strained patience as I
extolled the virtues of my classical music utopia, and then
immediately dismissed it as "sheer nonsense":

"Mr. Cui, you really need to read more. Where did this
ridiculous idea come from? You know, by day the Nazis
sent thousands of Jews to the furnaces without batting an
eyelash—they even tossed in newborn babies. But that
never prevented them from kicking back in the evenings
with their coffee while listening to Mozart or Chopin.
Plenty of those Nazi executioners were themselves brilliant
musicians, but did that ever inspire the tiniest expression of
goodness or compassion while they murdered people *en
masse*? You're a hi-fi guy, you must have heard of Furtwängler, right? The moment capitalism takes root, it creates its

own hero. When that hero emerges in the National Socialist Party, it's Hitler. When it emerges within a new capitalist economy, it's an all-devouring monster. And when it emerges in music, it's Beethoven. Obviously, Beethoven and Hitler are not one and the same, though the distinction between the two isn't as clear as most people imagine. Can you see now why I like Renaissance and Baroque music? In my opinion, society after the Baroque period is just a humongous pile of shit. I gave up on classical music after that period a long time ago.

"The fact that, like you said, you've never come across any cheating in the hi-fi community is no evidence at all that the people in it are more civilized or have better character, nor does it prove that their morals are superior in any way. All we can say is that you've been relatively lucky. And in a filthy, mediocre world, luck is the only religion. You've imagined the hi-fi community to be some sort of secret, egalitarian paradise, and you're free to believe that if you wish. But if you want to continue with your business, I advise you to be a little more careful. Caution is always best. No telling when bad luck might come knocking on your door."

Given my thick skull and poor memory, I can't be sure I've recounted what Bai Cheng'en said word-for-word, but that was the gist of it. After accepting his chastisement, my face turned crimson and I felt pathetic—you can probably visualize the whole scene. Although I'm a fairly stubborn guy, I'm definitely not the kind who's deaf to criticism. I mulled over what the counselor said for months, and listened to all nine of Beethoven's symphonies, as well as the late quartets, from start to finish. In the end, I had to admit that my life might be beyond hope.

It was impossible for me not to like Beethoven.

But Bai Cheng'en's admonitions caused another very different but obvious side effect. From then on, every time I wired money to a seller, I would always be as careful as I could. I feared that the bad luck the counselor had prophesied would suddenly fall upon my head.

It was precisely that fear which made me break into a cold sweat as I wired payment for the Linn 12 to the seller in Tongzhou.

I already mentioned that sixty-eight thousand yuan totaled practically my whole savings. I wired it to the account he had given me, but heard nothing for three straight days. I called him repeatedly, but he sounded irritated when we spoke and was always traveling—now way down south in Guizhou, now far northwest in Inner Mongolia. Then I couldn't even get through to him: either his phone was turned off, or I got the "We're sorry, the subscriber you have dialed is unavailable right now."

I asked Songping what to do. He told me to stop wasting time and call the police. Next I gritted my teeth and asked Bai Cheng'en's advice. I fully expected him to take the opportunity to sneer at my idiocy. But instead, he quietly considered it for a moment, then suggested against calling the police for now. He told me to calm down and wait a few more days. Needless to say, the counselor's advice once again proved correct.

The very day I completed work on the 845 amplifier, the seller of the Linn 12 phoned me. He said he was standing at the front door of my apartment building, holding the machine. Clearly the impetuous type. He said he had just come back from Benxi, up in Manchuria, and apologized profusely for the late delivery. He even brought me some of the local specialties he had bought during his the trip: a bag of pine nuts, a bag of hazelnuts, and a small bottle of walnut oil. After carrying the machine upstairs, out of courtesy I asked if he'd like to join me for dinner. He readily agreed. While we ate, he got up "to hit the head," and ended up paying the check.

Later discoveries further indicated that he really was an upstanding guy. The ad he had posted online for the machine promised its condition as "95% new," but when I lifted it out of the soft plastic wrapping I could see it might as well have arrived straight from the factory. The pale gray metal body emanated a chilly sheen along with a strong sharp smell. This marked my first intimate contact with a Lotus 12 player. You may have heard the other nickname audiophiles have bestowed on it: The Drug.

I must admit that I was pretty excited. I plugged the power cord into the adapter, connected the adapter to the 845, then linked the Autograph speakers with my Vovox cables. I hurried along so quick that I sliced my finger on the adapter's wire housing. The hour neared ten o'clock— the patter of footsteps and the crying of children from other apartments had faded away. I couldn't wait to hear how the full system would sound. The half hour it took to warm up felt interminably long.

While I waited, my sister called.

As soon as she opened her mouth, nothing could shut her up. She asked over and over what I thought of Hou Meizhu. She wrongfully interpreted my reluctance to answer as shyness. The truth was I didn't want to ruin my mood before trying out the new system, so I suppressed my anger and chose my words carefully; she took it as a green light to push me harder, even to the point of telling me to strike while the iron was hot and go fill out the marriage registration forms with Hou Meizhu that weekend. She drove me over the edge.

"Go fuck your mother!" I yelled into the phone.

"Ei, ei, ei, what kind of language is that?! My mother? And who's your mother, then?"

8. SATIE, THE GNOSSIENNES

DING CAICHEN lived in an area called Sleeping Dragon Valley, on the border of Tianjin and Pinggu, though technically a suburb of the former. I took Fushi Road out to the West Fifth Ring Road and circled north, merging onto the Airport Expressway and on to the Beijing-Pinggu highway, which starts next to Terminal 3.

As Ding Caichen's directions indicated, exactly an hour and a half later I entered a fairly short tunnel, before coming to a tollbooth in Tian Valley, at which I paid twenty-five yuan, then turned onto an empty mountain road.

Autumn was coming to an end. The various deciduous trees—sumacs, maples, smoke trees, dawn redwoods—had been turned a deeper red by the frost. The entire mountain range shone with their colors—not only a pure red, but a collage of deep purples, browns, and bright yellows. This must be what native Beijingers refer to when they talk about the "mountain brocade" that only appears in late autumn. Who knew that such a beautiful place could be hidden away in the suburbs of Beijing! As I wound down the narrow mountain road, a feeling of awe washed over me, as well as feelings of sorrow and resentment for being excluded. You can't help but admire the sense of smell the wealthy possess. Even at the edges of a foul, trash-infested city, they always find a way to hunt down the last patches of pristine territory and claim them as their own.

At a deserted fork in the road, I came to the massive billboard where Ding Caichen had agreed to meet me: it displayed the phrase "Development is the only way" on top of a not particularly true-to-life profile portrait of Deng Xiaoping. Ding Caichen waited for me in a black Volkswagen sedan parked directly under the billboard. He didn't get out of his car, but merely hit the horn twice and beckoned with a wave from his window. I followed him down a mountain lane heading east, and after twenty minutes, we turned onto an even narrower road that skirted a golf course.

If you've ever been to the art districts in the Beijing suburbs, like 789 or The Distillery, it will be easy for you to imagine the style of the houses in Sleeping Dragon Valley. Lots of red brick walls; long, asymmetrical lines of windows; cylindrical water towers and exposed steel I beams. If not for the fancy cars that decorated the driveways, you might think you had wandered into a 1950s factory district. Scattered over the gentle mountain slopes, the buildings lay low amid forests of naked trees, their elaborate design masked by outward simplicity, their masterful detail peeping out from crude wilderness. Seen from far off, they looked less like high-end residential spaces than random piles of lumber.

Ding Caichen appeared to be over forty; fairly thin and not very tall; face tired, slightly sickly. He wore a black zip-up turtleneck sweater and gray corduroy pants. The beard on his split-rail face didn't really stand out. His small, round eyes appeared close together behind the tea-colored lenses of his spectacles.

Every so often he would sniff audibly.

I reached out a hand with instinctive cordiality, just as I realized that he had no intention of shaking it. By then it was too late, and so to avoid embarrassment I grabbed his right hand and gave it a symbolic wag—it felt soft and feeble. Yet for the most part I didn't sense anything mysterious about him, at least nothing that might instill fear. His occasional smiles even betrayed a sort of awkward shyness. I couldn't understand why Jiang Songping had behaved so strangely when he described him to me.

Ding Caichen asked me about my drive, where I had come from, whether the six-car accident that had occurred that morning in the tunnel had been cleaned up or not. Other questions followed of the standard small-talk variety. Then he waved to a couple of security guards patrolling nearby. The guards understood immediately, left their patrols and jogged over to us. "We'll go in and have a cup of tea first," Ding Caichen said to me. "They'll handle the stuff in the car." He started walking.

I hurriedly reminded him that two guards might not be enough to lift the boxes; he merely waved a hand and replied, without turning around, "Don't worry about it. They'll think of something."

I followed him through a small wooden door to the north end of the grounds. We walked down a narrow cobblestone path around a copse of tallow trees blackened by frost, ascended three or four stone steps, and arrived at the house's eastern gate. Along both sides of this tiered walkway ran a narrow corridor filled with flowers and shrubs that extended into the courtyard.

The first thing that struck me about the house was how its architecture created an intensely private environment.

The raised entryway lead to a sunken living room, dining room, and kitchen, seamlessly divided into three independent units by low walls and screens. A full-length picture window in the living room provided excellent natural sunlight, and the high perimeter wall outside prevented any hopeful passersby from peering into the house, while those inside still enjoyed a full view of the colorful outdoor scenery.

In a previous telephone conversation, I had asked Ding Caichen to describe the layout of his living room. The floor-to-ceiling window on the south side worried me. As I'm sure you know, glass is terrible at containing sound. Sound waves bounce off the glass to create interference that ruins the final stereo imaging effect. Ding Caichen followed my advice and installed a thick curtain in front of the south wall. As you can see, Ding Caichen clearly seemed to be a reasonable man, open to suggestions. His living room, though spacious, didn't provide a favorable listening environment for enjoying music. Usually the best place to position a speaker would be along the shortest wall of a room. But the shortest walls in this room were on the east and west ends, and they had no empty space. The west wall was occupied by a tower air conditioner, which couldn't be moved easily, and next to it a colossal fish tank, complete with softly undulating water plants and two eel-like animals (I learned later these were actually prized Arowana fish) swimming back and forth. An egg-shaped sun room was built along the eastern wall of the living room. Also not a good place to put a sound system, especially given the wooden lounge chair and circular nightstand taking up the space.

I noticed a tray atop the side table with a coffee mug,

book, and two sky-blue hairpins on it. It seemed reasonable to conclude that the lady of the house had just been here reading a book or basking in the sun, and had left before we entered.

By the time they hauled the pair of bulky Autograph speakers into the living room, the number of security guards had increased from two to six. Ding Caichen instructed them to place the speakers down in front of the window that served as the southern wall. Yet this would position them too close to the sofa, negatively affecting the projection of sound. I didn't mention this to Ding Caichen. Though he seemed like a calm, amiable person, I had noticed his eyebrows constantly knitting together in a pensive manner, and he wasn't saying much.

As I prepared to test my creation, I asked him if it would be all right to draw the curtains. He took a quiet drag on his cigarette, then looked at me and replied softly, "Oh... whatever you like."

His voice, tired and weak, possessed none of the impatient eagerness you'd expect from an audiophile about to test out a new sound system. With slight disappointment, I asked him to move toward the center of the sofa, so that his ears would line up in an equilateral triangle with the two speakers.

He froze for a second, as if stunned, then did as I asked.

In order to lighten the mood a little, I proudly described the remarkable features of the machinery, emphasizing its legendary reputation in the audiophile world. As to whether or not you can call it the world's finest sound system, I said to him, I couldn't be sure, but it was absolutely the best I had ever heard. I admitted half-jokingly that I had held on to the speakers for twelve whole years, never able to part with them. I had feelings for them, I said, sort of like the way you'd feel toward a daughter, or lover.

"That would be incest, wouldn't it?" Ding Caichen looked up at me and forced a smile.

I had brought three test CDs with me. The first a piano recording, naturally, to test the system's differentiation capacity as well as the purity of the sound. The second Cecilia Bartoli singing Donizetti, to show my Autographs' new owner the unbelievable fullness and subtle sound quality produced by its dual concentric core. The last a 1990 Chesky recording of Antal Dorati conducting the Royal Philharmonic in "Dance of the Seven Veils," from Richard Strauss's *Salome*. Everyone knows this is a particularly valuable album, the work of the master recording engineer Kenneth Wilkinson in his prime.

I played three- to five-minute samples from each recording in consecutive order. I observed with considerable shock that Ding Caichen appeared to be tone-deaf. The music didn't move him at all. His face remained entirely expressionless, as if covered in wax. You can imagine the rage that boiled up within me. Besides the occasional sniff, he even picked up a newspaper from the coffee table, before putting it down after realizing the room was too dark to read in. Why a tone-deaf man should ask Jiang Songping to find him "the best sound system in the world" was a question I couldn't bring myself to pursue, due to my utter disappointment. My heart sank; I began to simply go through the motions of my work.

After I switched to the *Salome* recording, Ding Caichen surprised me by clearing his throat and asking, "Isn't this a little loud? Hmm? Don't you think? Can you play the other one again?"

Hearing this, I immediately stopped the frenetic orchestral dancing of *Salome* and returned to the beautiful Bartoli, the image of John the Baptist's head on a plate still floating before me.

"No, no, not this one," interjected Ding Caichen, "the first one, the piano piece."

So he wanted Pascal Rogé's performance.

Ding Caichen began to listen intently, and offered simple, sporadic appraisals of what he heard. He put on no airs of being an expert, speaking haltingly and without confidence. And yet, though I can't tell you exactly why, I couldn't help but feel that his general understanding of the music seemed accurate. As when he commented, "The piano's voice sounds like it's coming through a fog. I don't mean a thick, blinding fog—more like a thin, gauzy mist. Soft and indistinct. What do you think?"

"Yes, very possible."

"Who is this?"

"Satie, a French composer."

"Is he famous?"

"Hard to say." I adjusted the volume slightly and replied, "A lot of people secretly like his music."

"Why do you say 'secretly'?"

"Well, I mean, Satie's historical standing isn't very high. Most people who listen to music—here in China, I mean—don't really know him. I suppose I can't really say that now, as more and more people have been listening to him in recent years. I guess what I mean is that, historically speaking, he's been overlooked. You know, he was Debussy's teacher."

"And who is this Debussy?"

"Debussy? I just told you, Satie's student."

"I'm sorry, I know nothing about music." From his tone

it sounded like Ding Caichen's mood had elevated a bit. "What's the name of the piece we're listening to?"

"Gnossiennes."

"Doesn't it sound veiled in a mist?"

"You know, I can see a fog there. I had never noticed it before. If you like this CD, I can leave it here for you."

"No, that's all right," Ding Caichen said, hugging his arms, his voice once again chilly and restrained.

I'll be honest: by the time we had listened to the six Gnossiennes in sequential order, I had developed a real fondness for Ding Caichen. The man's knowledge of classical music was obviously poor—you could even call it complete ignorance. Yet his concentration and devout attention to the music as he listened impressed me. He acted nothing like your average audiophile, who talked big and put on a show of understanding when he understood nothing, for fear of being seen as an amateur; he disclosed no such egoism or pretense. For the duration of our listening, he sat on the couch with his upper body tilted slightly forward, hand on his chin, quiet as a sleeping baby. Even his habitual sniff had gone.

"Let me ask you this: If it weren't Rogé playing, but someone else, would the performance be very different?" Ding Caichen drew back the curtains to let the sunlight in from the courtyard. He held the CD in his hands and examined both sides of it as he spoke.

"Well, sure, that goes without saying. If it had been Lang Lang playing that piece, the misty aura you just heard might not have been present at all. Different performers will always interpret a piece very differently."

"Fine, fine . . . so, besides Satie, are there any other composers with similar styles that I could listen to?"

I thought for a moment, then told him that if he liked this type of music, the pupil of Satie's I had previously mentioned, Debussy, definitely would be worth listening to, particularly his Images series and the 24 Preludes. Chopin's nocturnes and Haydn's piano sonatas would also be good choices.

"Fine, fine ... And what's a harpsichord?"

"The harpsichord is the forefather of the modern piano. Some call it the 'ancient piano.' Do you like the harpsichord?" I couldn't help but look up and examine this mysterious man who so terrified Jiang Songping.

"I've never heard it before. Just a random question."

Ding Caichen looked nervously at his watch, sniffed hard, and asked with a slight frown that if I wasn't in a hurry to get home, would I be able to stay for lunch. The invitation sounded forced; I imagined he hoped I'd refuse.

Still, I agreed without hesitation. You can probably guess the reason why.

He added that no one in the house cooked, so we'd have to go out to eat. He had a place in mind some distance away. I made my way to the bathroom before we left.

As I passed the foot of the staircase, around a basin filled with Asiatic lilies, I heard the sound of a woman coughing upstairs. Whether this was Ding Caichen's wife, his daughter, or somebody else, I had no idea. Two more coughs followed. When I came out of the bathroom, I couldn't help glancing up the stairway, then over to Ding Caichen. I considered suggesting that he call down the person upstairs to join us for lunch.

He was changing his footwear by the doorway; he slipped out of his loafers—standard wear for any Beijinger —and grabbed a gray windbreaker from the rack. Then he turned to me and smiled, saying, "I'm sorry, I forgot to mention it before. I'll wire the remaining two hundred and sixty thousand into your account immediately. No need to worry, I have your account number."

Hearing this, I felt a little pang of regret. If he had only brought this up a few minutes earlier, there would have been no reason for me to stay for lunch.

We arrived at a Hunan restaurant next to the real-estate development office. The pungent smell of old chili oil permeated the air inside. We picked a table and sat down. It was still early, and for the moment we had the place to ourselves. At the service counter, five or six members of the wait staff crowded together, chattering quietly in Hunanese.

After a little while, a chubby waitress sauntered over to our table with a menu under her arm. Ding Caichen accepted the menu from her, flipped through it carelessly, and said, "Let's have a pot of tea first—Pu'erh tea. And bring me an ashtray, please."

"There's no smoking in here," she abruptly replied.

Ding Caichen looked up; he pushed his glasses up the bridge of his nose and stared at her for a second, as if he didn't understand what she had just said. Then he gave a short chuckle, and repeated in a low voice, "It's fine. Just bring me an ashtray."

"I'm sorry, sir, smoking isn't allowed in public places, it's the law. I hope you'll understand. I'm sorry, if you really feel the need to …"

The chubby waitress couldn't finish her sentence. Ding Caichen had reached into the pocket of his windbreaker to remove a solid black object, which he placed gently on the tabletop.

It was a handgun.

Ding Caichen's gaunt, ashen face turned savage. "Savage" isn't exactly the right word, because the darkness that suddenly clouded his face clearly stemmed from an unconcealed, magnified anguish. He looked terrifying; I could plainly see that the frail little man could completely lose it at any moment.

I had never seen a real handgun before. My terror muffled another sentiment—I felt an irresistible urge to reach out and touch the weapon. Truthfully, I could barely believe what was happening, even with the gun lying there right under my nose. By the time I snapped out of my prolonged moment of shock, I noticed the chubby waitress had disappeared.

Everyone had cleared out—the restaurant was now deserted.

A few moments later, a man rushed from the back of the restaurant to our table, where he bowed and apologized, nodding and smiling obsequiously. He looked about fifty and called himself the manager. He referred to Ding Caichen, at least twenty years his junior, as "Uncle Ding" (so they were already acquainted); the chubby waitress, whom he called "that stupid little bitch," was his niece, a recent migrant from the countryside. The manager kept asking us to move to one of the private rooms. Ding Caichen, however, didn't say a word, so the manager dropped it. Then he started to plead with Ding Caichen to put "that baby" on the table away—more guests would be arriving, you know, no need for it to be out in the open. Ding Caichen remained silent, as if engulfed by some sort of excruciating agony, and totally ignored the manager's well-intentioned requests. After a long, awkward pause, the manager could only cover the gun with a yellow cloth napkin.

In a flash, dishes of all kinds materialized on the table, along with two crystal ashtrays and a pack of expensive Nanjing cigarettes.

Yet, strangely, Ding Caichen didn't smoke a single one throughout the entire course of the meal. He didn't eat much, and he spoke even less. Of course, the handgun under the napkin made me desperate to leave as soon as possible; when he did speak, I could hardly focus my attention to formulate a response. On the drive home, as I entered the tunnel, I suddenly recalled Ding Caichen asking me if I could come take a look at the sound system if he experienced any problems with it. This is more or less what I could remember saying to him: "Sure, that goes without saying. People in my line of work fetishize the machine to a degree. Normal folks would definitely find us a little weird. You know, you sell off a nice piece of equipment, but you never really let it go. It feels like marrying off your daughter, no exaggeration. You can no longer protect her or care for her, and you secretly hope the new owner will be as good to her as you had been. Even though you know she's already married, you still can't resist the impulse to go see her. All audiophiles are like this; others don't understand it. Thus, if I could have the opportunity to return to your home and see her again, that would be more than I could ask for."

Ding Caichen gave me an absent-minded thank you, then looked me in the eyes for a long time without saying anything. The expression on his face suggested that he was making multiple calculations simultaneously. Finally, perhaps unable to think of anything else to say, he brought up the subject of money again. He smiled wanly and said, "Don't worry, I will wire the rest of the money to your account. A man like me doesn't have many good points, but I do stand by my word. In this world, anything can happen, but that two hundred sixty thousand will be paid to you, down to the last cent."

You can guess the first thing I did when I returned home from Sleeping Dragon Valley that afternoon. I downloaded the horror movie *Her Lost Soul* and watched it from beginning to end. But really, I only needed to see the first few minutes to figure it out.

I mean, to figure out why Jiang Songping had randomly brought it up the first time he described Ding Caichen.

9. RED DAWN

Two days passed.

Two weeks passed.

A month passed.

The two hundred and sixty thousand yuan Ding Caichen promised he would wire me never posted to my account. I could feel something was wrong, though I had no way of knowing what. I toughed it out for a few more anxious days, then with shaking fingers dialed his cell number. An unfamiliar voice came on the line. The guy spoke with a thick Sha'anxi accent—definitely couldn't be Ding Caichen.

"What do you want?" he demanded in greeting. I couldn't finish explaining my concerns before he completely blew up: "You're right messed up, huh? You got a fuckin' death wish, huh?"

Then he hung up.

After that, I tried several times to muster the courage to call back, but I couldn't do it. And I couldn't figure out what the hell "messed up" referred to, either. I could only bother my old friend Jiang Songping once again.

"What did I tell you, brother? I said you had to be extra careful dealing with the likes of him, and now look what's happened." He lowered his voice and continued, "And let me tell you, I'm in as big a mess as you are right now. My goddamn senile mother has gotten it into her head that I should take her to the Maldives. Yeah, anything you fucking want, Ma. Fucking hell. Let me call you back in a bit. . . ."

He never called back.

One windy afternoon in December, the bastard Chang Baoguo slouched his way into my apartment, dragging his bad leg behind him. I tried my best to explain my situation to him, but no matter what I said, he just looked at me with suspicion and disappointment, shaking his head and sighing. As if I myself had done something shameful. He demanded that I give him a firm date for moving out, so he wouldn't lose his patience. A clear enough threat, but to make sure I fully understood he put it in more obvious terms. He claimed he had "done everything he could for me," and that "a man's patience was actually very, very, very limited." A piece of shit like him could be capable of anything.

One definite piece of information I gathered, which he repeated several times amid a steady stream of profanity, was that this problem, without question, could not drag on into the new year. Nothing to be done—he wanted me out before the end of the year. Anger, panic, and desperation caused my head to spin; I took a deep breath and reassured him that December thirty-first would be fine. That left me only three or four days. He forced me to put it in writing.

A copse of birch trees and a transformer station bordered my apartment building. Standing on my bedroom balcony, I watched Chang Baoguo hobble his way to the edge of the trees, and suddenly halt. He lit a cigarette, then waved a hand toward the thickest section of the grove, next to the station shed. A small figure emerged from behind the wall and ran to him. She glanced up in my direction. The two of them clung to each other for support, and soon limped off across the road like a dinghy in rough seas. When they reached the sign for the 356 bus, they stopped and waited.

For the first time in my life, I discovered that my wrinkled old sister was a pretty funny woman indeed.

Though I knew it would hardly make a difference, I decided to sell the rest of my hi-fi equipment at significantly discounted prices online, as a one-time clearance sale. I would have sold myself to defray moving costs had anyone asked. I didn't have to wait long for my first buyer to appear.

Colonel Shen, a military commander, had his heart set on my Red Dawn flat-line speaker cables.

Early one evening, Colonel Shen arrived at my place in a Humvee, cash in hand, ready to pick up his merchandise. He told me he had decided to buy this particular pair of cables because his new wife liked the name: Red Dawn. He said that using them to listen to music made you think of a red sun rising in a fountain of light.

I supposed that when times are tough it can be easy to become a little unhinged. Shit. Colonel Shen had barely walked through the door and for whatever reason I just started to babble on about Ding Caichen, the epic sound system, the missing money. I poured out my heart out to some soldier I had never met before. I knew how undignified it looked, exposing my own weaknesses to a stranger, but for some unfathomable reason, I simply couldn't control myself, as if a sympathetic God had sent me an angel to hear my misfortune.

Though I described Ding Caichen several times as an in-timidating and mysterious figure, I withheld the part about the pistol on the table. Tall and muscular, Colonel Shen possessed an open, trustworthy face. Even the pockmarks on his cheeks made me feel safer. He listened to my entire tale with cool patience, then smiled dismissively and growled, "Aren't you being a little too sensitive, Mr. Cui? Nothing in your story sounds particularly terrifying to me. For a buyer to delay payment or even refuse it altogether is common enough, whether for financial reasons or some-thing else. It's no big deal. Worst-case scenario, you can al-ways take him to court. If you can't reach him by phone, you should drive back out there, find this guy Ding, and ask him what's going on. That would be better than sitting here, making yourself miserable."

He must have noticed the timidity in my expression, as he added in a half-joking tone, "Guys like you just love dwelling inside your own head. If you're really worried something will happen, why don't I send over a couple of armed soldiers here tomorrow to go with you?"

I thanked him for his generous offer, but declined. Still, his words confirmed a fear that had been slowly growing in my mind: I really had no other choice but to drive back to Sleeping Dragon Valley.

10. LEONHARDT

WHEN I left my apartment that morning, a steady rain fell from a thick, gray sky. I say rain, but it felt more like sleet. The heavy, glittering droplets were piercingly cold, as if they might transform into a flurry of snowflakes in a moment. As my car entered the mountains, the steady rain turned into a downpour, an endless curtain of hammering raindrops that flooded the pavement of the deserted highway.

Beijing usually didn't have such heavy rains this early in the winter. Those paranoid scholars and professors would have something to say about it. As everyone knows, they're capable of interpreting any natural disaster, any abnormality in the climate or seasons, as a sign that the world is coming to an end. Every day they're online claiming this or disputing that, as if they were indubitable experts at how to run the country. They produce opinions like a dysfunctional endocrine system secreting hormones, or like a senseless fog building up layer after layer, or like measles, in hot flashes followed by chills. If you're stupid enough to take them seriously, you gradually realize that you can't even figure out what they're trying to say!

So for instance, you hear them constantly droning on about how the Three Gorges Dam caused the earthquake in Sichuan; how a rapid rise in ocean temperature caused the southeastern tsunami; how various gases trapped beneath the ocean floor would kill ninety percent of the population if they ever broke out to the earth's surface. The logical conclusion would be to reduce our carbon footprint, and yet if you ask these people to use a little less electricity, or to decrease their driving, it's as if you're robbing them at gunpoint. They seem incapable of doing anything but complaining. If the number of mosquitoes dropped one summer, they'd say, My God, the world's gotten so bad even the mosquitoes can't adapt. And if the mosquito population boomed, they'd say, Shit, it looks like only mosquitoes can thrive in this world. One of my clients regurgitated the most ridiculous theory I had ever heard. His research focused on "joint friction" or something like that. He had just returned from Tubingen; claimed to be a vegetarian. He thought the biggest contributor to global warming wasn't car exhaust nor industrial pollution, but cow farts. He liked to use the phrase "in point of fact" a lot, I couldn't say why.

Even if what these so-called experts say sounds reasonable, I still think they're fabricating a lot of it. More importantly, if what they say turns out to be true, how could it possibly relate to a poor man about to be kicked out of his home by his own sister? If the world's ending, let it end, I thought. I didn't have the energy to care about questions of such magnitude.

Only one concrete problem dominated my limited, selfish imagination, namely, how to get the two hundred and sixty thousand yuan Ding Caichen owed me as painlessly as possible so I could move out of my apartment and into that farmer's courtyard by the end of the year, and in the process salvage what little dignity I had left. I couldn't endure being humiliated by a piece of shit like Chang Baoguo for the rest of my life.

I parked my car outside of Ding Caichen's courtyard.

After I turned the ignition off, I could hear the sound of music drifting from inside the house. It seemed to me an unmistakable sign: Ding Caichen was still listening to music and so nothing could be wrong, all would be well. I could tell that full, flawless piano timbre emanated from my Autograph speakers—no doubt about it. I also recognized the recording: Emil Gilels playing Brahms's second piano concerto, his 1972 performance with Eugen Jochum and the Berlin Philharmonic. Of all the piano concertos ever composed, Brahms's second has been my favorite by far. I think of it as my Requiem. In my opinion, not even Beethoven's "Emperor" Concerto reaches the same heights. So I sat in the car, listening to the third movement, my somber mood brightening up. The northern winds wailing by outside couldn't dispel the warmth the music brought me. It caused me to forget my predicament, and stirred a long-suppressed pride in my handiwork.

That a person should live his entire life without the opportunity to enjoy such beautiful music would be a shame!

I walked along the curving, mud-veined stone path as I had before to the north end of the house. I found the red doorbell on the wooden gate and pressed it. The music faded in and out without stopping—no one answered the door. I gave the bell a lingering, persistent second ring, then a short, perfunctory third. Finally, the door on the east side of the house opened; a woman wearing a floral-patterned jacket and a headscarf came out the door and down the steps, a spring-green umbrella open in her hand.

The silk scarf wrapped around her head covered her face completely, leaving only a narrow slit for her eyes. Her appearance made me think of a conservative Arab woman in a burqa, or a headscarved Chechen terrorist. As she neared and looked me up and down, I admit that my heart skipped a few beats.

From the other side of the gate, I introduced myself and explained my business with Ding Caichen. I remarked with feigned cheerfulness that the music she had been enjoying was being played on a sound system I had designed especially for her home. She paused for a minute before finally opening the wooden gate.

When I took off my shoes inside the front door, I remembered that I hadn't put on clean socks; my leather shoes were soaked from the rain, and the smell from my feet truly exceeded the descriptive borders of the word "putrid." Afraid of offending her, I didn't put on the slippers offered me, but instead grabbed a pair of loafers from the shoe rack above, with the hope of blocking the stench that poured forth in waves from my feet.

But the woman stopped me. She told me to use a pair of slippers by the door.

Drenched, with stinking feet, I decided not to sit down, for fear of staining her furniture.

"Is Ding Caichen out?" I asked her. The woman walked over to the expansive window and turned off the Linn 12. The room suddenly became very quiet.

"He is gone."

"Oh, then do you know when he'll be back?" I continued. "Could I possibly wait for him here?"

"He is gone," she repeated. Though we were now inside, she still hadn't removed the silk scarf around her head, which intensified my uneasiness.

If you had been there yourself, and heard her repeat "He is gone" in that tone, would your heart have started to pound as you wondered what the hell "gone" was supposed to fucking mean? Would you have secretly suspected, though you yourself didn't want to believe it, that Ding Caichen, this mystery man who could pull a pistol out of his pocket as if it were a pack of cigarettes, who gave Jiang Songping shivers at the mere mention of his name, was now, definitively, motherfucking dead?

Well, you would have been right.

The woman told me that Ding Caichen had jumped off a thirty-story office building in Dongzhimen last week, a cup of coffee still in his hand.

Simple as that.

The shock of hearing this forced me to push my own concerns aside for a moment, temporarily suppressing my desire to collect my two hundred and sixty thousand yuan. I automatically picked a copy of the *Beijing News* from the coffee table, spread it out on a sofa cushion, and sat down.

The offhand way in which the woman described the circumstances of Ding Caichen's death deepened my apprehensiveness toward her. Still, I tacitly reminded myself that asking about her relationship to Ding Caichen might be a little too abrupt for the moment. But my excessive caution, caught as I was in a dizzying state between agitation and fear, led me inadvertently to commit an even bigger error. I breathed in sharply and asked her, "I'm sorry, I know I shouldn't ask you this, but why is your face wrapped up?"

She paused, then replied, "I don't like it this way either. If you're not squeamish, I'll take it off now. But you need to be sure."

Honestly, I didn't understand what she meant. My brain extended so far into the absurd that I even imagined her to be Ding Caichen himself, feigning a woman's voice and appearance, covering his face just to play some kind of sick joke on me.

I can't remember how I responded. What I do remember is her turning around to take off the brown silk scarf, and then, with a jerk, swinging back to face me again.

I stared at a violently disfigured face.

If you're ever fortunate enough to see her face, I'm sure you'll recognize as I did that the damage wasn't caused by acid or some other corrosive liquid, but by a metal blade. Innumerable slashes in every direction had healed into a cross-hatched web of raised and uneven scars. I'm not sure how to describe her face as a whole, except that each slash silently replayed the sequence of its own mutilation.

If you've ever seen someone who has suffered severe cowpox, you know how flesh looks that's been gouged and then scarred over. At the top of her cheekbone beneath her left eye I could make out a triangular hole, which, despite evidence of reconstructive surgery, still looked prominent and deep. A long scar along her right jawline stretched in a diagonal curve to the base of her ear; you could see the dot-and-dash marks left by the stitches. At first glance, it resembled a scorpion waving his tail. One of her nostrils was no more than a ragged hole.

Later I learned that a knife hadn't caused the injury to

her nostril; her nose had been partly chewed off by human teeth. The missing bit of flesh hadn't been found, either, suggesting that her tormentor had simply swallowed it. A piece of her lip had also been mutilated the same way, so that her two front teeth remained exposed when she closed her mouth. The sheer, revolting ugliness of her face contrasted sharply with her fair, long neck, reminding me of a withered camellia—stem and leaves still bright green and vigorous, the flower wasted away and black.

"You said you were here about the sound system, sir?" she asked. "Did he not pay you?"

"He paid me a portion—a hundred thirty thousand." I gave her an awkward smile.

"Well, what was the total price?"

"Three hundred and ninety."

"I see. That's why you've come."

I didn't know whether to look at her or look away. Staring straight at her certainly wouldn't have been very polite; but for me to fix my gaze elsewhere and purposefully avoid looking at her would be rude, too. Thankfully, she turned away again, this time to gaze out the window.

The rain continued to pound on the roof and the wind picked up.

After several minutes of silence, she said, "How about this: if you return the hundred and thirty thousand, you can just take back the sound system."

I told her that her suggestion seemed perfectly fair, but my current situation simply couldn't handle it. Put yourself in my shoes for a second: I had already spent my entire savings just to buy the Linn 12 from the seller in Tongzhou. If I were to take her offer... even putting aside the fact that the courtyard I wanted so badly would go up in smoke, and that shithead Chang Baoguo's deadline was almost upon me . . . forget about all that . . . if I agreed to her plan and returned the hundred and thirty thousand in exchange for my own sound system, wouldn't it not only mean that I had finished two months of work for no profit, but also that I had spent sixty-eight thousand yuan on a Linn 12 I would never use myself? If you had been me, would you have agreed to it?

It seemed necessary to tell her the whole story of my sister and the forced move, so as to give her a clear understanding of the big picture, while also maybe triggering a little sympathy in the process. When I finished, I thought I had explained everything as plainly as possible, but the woman seemed confused, or unconvinced. Of course I couldn't expect a person of her economic status to be able to empathize with a poor bastard like me.

"If you'd like to leave it here, that would be great for me. He knew I loved music, which is why he ordered it from you before he killed himself. I'm definitely no audiophile! I used to listen to music on ordinary computer speakers. But the first time I tried your sound system, I fell totally in love with it. It just has . . . I don't know . . . its voice has such colorful resonance. So it would be hard for me to let it go. What about this: The money you don't have to worry about. Though his company accounts were frozen after he died, it's only a temporary situation. The company needs to pay off his debts, then his remaining assets need to be audited. I don't have enough money to pay you back right now, but I can guarantee that as soon as the auditing is completed, I'll pay you in full. I can even calculate a little interest to add to it. You have the initial hundred thirty thousand, right? Why not rent a place and move in there for the time being?"

It looked like my best option, and truth be told, I had

considered the possibility before. But could I actually find another apartment within three days? It seemed unlikely. After I voiced this concern, she turned back to me and smiled (if you can call the mechanical movement of her lips a smile): "I have another idea. If you're really stuck and don't think you'll be able to find a place, you can always live here for a while. I'm on my own, and this house is too big for me alone."

Obviously she must be kidding, I thought to myself.

And if not, I didn't think I could bear living with that face. As she spoke, another idea popped into my head that soothed my mood considerably. I recalled I still had in my possession a golden ticket: a promise that my old friend Jiang Songping had once made to me.

Before I left her house, I asked her a nagging question that I hadn't dared to bring up yet: What could've made Ding Caichen so distraught he would decide to end his own life?

"Oh, he wasn't distraught." She corrected me in the same matter-of-fact tone, as if talking about a total stranger. "If you ask me, I think he jumped because he finally figured it out. He should've jumped a long time ago."

"What I meant was, I find it hard to believe that someone like Ding Caichen would commit suicide...."

"Even the South Korean president committed suicide, what's so hard to believe?" She opened the front door for me. As she watched me put on my shoes, something seemed to dawn on her.

"I'm sorry, but do you know where I could find Gustav Leonhardt's recordings? Specifically, his harpsichord performance of Bach's Goldberg Variations."

The question astonished me. Not exactly the most popular album. I'd say only a precious few, a handful of audiophiles, in China had ever heard it.

"I doubt you can find it on the open market. But I happen to have a copy at home. If you write down your address, I can have a courier bring it to you tomorrow."

She thanked me, found a pen and paper, and wrote down her address. She also called my cell phone, so we could get in touch more easily.

Before I met up with my dear old friend again, I had put a growing measure of hope upon his shoulders. I planned to pose my request for help as a choice: First, to ask him for a two hundred thousand yuan loan. If it worked, that amount plus Ding Caichen's hundred and thirty thousand would be enough for me to move into the courtyard house today or tomorrow. Or second, to persuade him to buy the entire sound system himself. Not until six or seven years after Mou Qishan's estate auction did he find out about the bargain I had finagled. Once he did, he told me with a palpable envy that if it hadn't been for his diarrhea, those Autograph speakers would be his. Once, he even offered to buy them from me for three times the price I had paid.

Whichever option he chose would fix my dilemma perfectly. My confidence brimmed, too, because of something Songping said to me twenty-five years ago.

It was the winter of 1984, during my time as an apprentice at Red Capital Apparel. Jiang Songping accidentally impregnated the prettiest lass at the Telecommunications College. He ran over to the ready-made apparel department, yanked me into a corner by the men's room, and pleaded with me, stamping his feet and clenching his hands, to help him figure out what to do.

At the time, getting a woman pregnant out of wedlock crossed my moral bottom line, to say nothing of the fact that she wasn't even the steady girlfriend he had been bringing around to show off to me. He put me in a tough spot. But I knew very well what the college would do to him if they found out, being, as he was, a probationary member of the Communist Party. I had no choice but to put aside my own exalted morals. I decided to take the two of them secretly to Yancheng, and ask my uncle there to help her get an abortion.

In order to solidify the ruse, Jiang Songping asked me to do something so outlandish I could hardly believe it: he wanted me to pretend to be the "it" girl's boyfriend. As I was a nobody, he argued, not subordinate to any organization or institution, if the news ever got out it wouldn't have any major "political consequences."

His concerns, in the end, seemed justified. I decided true altruism didn't quit halfway, and I went along with his crazy idea.

With my uncle's help, the "it" girl underwent a D&C procedure without complications. My animated aunt cooked her chicken soup every day until she recovered, while my uncle spent the equivalent of two months' salary to buy her an expensive wool coat. Songping accepted the coat without hesitation, commenting, "Those in crisis don't quibble over details"; the "it" girl even tried it on, sashaying in front of a mirror.

Still a student, Songping didn't have much cash on hand;

I basically covered all their expenses, including train tickets, food, and admission tickets for a few tourist attractions in Yangzhou.

On the train home to Beijing, with his arm around his dozing girlfriend, Songping made me a slow and solemn promise.

"Brother, I am truly in debt to you. Remember, if there ever comes a day when you have to move a mountain, just ask me, and I'll lay down my life to move it for you."

The next day I called him seven or eight times, but he never picked up. I finally tracked him down that afternoon in the executive conference room of Textile Tower on Minzhuang Road.

He stepped out of a meeting with his Board of Directors to come talk to me. A retailer in Tianjin had just sent back a shipment due to quality issues, putting him in a frenzied state. With understandable annoyance, he glared at me, ordering me to "Spit it out!" in a voice that boiled over with impatience.

This wasn't the Songping I knew. I was caught completely off-guard.

With a darkened face, Songping controlled himself long enough to hear my explanation, before berating me in a way I had never seen before:

"Are you not finished being a pain in my ass? Are you retarded, or just fucking clueless? What business did you have telling that woman about the initial payment? Ding Caichen's fucking dead, there's no paper trail, how could she know if you hadn't told her? If you had just shown up and carted the machinery home, you could've kept the money and rented a place anywhere you like. But now look at you, running to me for money while I'm pulling strings to beg the bank for a loan! I don't have any money, but even if I fucking did, I couldn't give you any! Let me ask you a question: are we brothers or not?"

Stunned, I didn't say a word. Shouldn't I have been the one asking that question? I swallowed my anger and nodded.

"That's more like it. Now how can brothers bring up money so carelessly? 'Men have kin, gold has none,' that's the law! Don't you understand the law? It's supposed to be something you just know without talking about, but you're forcing me to explain it—I hope you're happy."

"Well, but I...I mean I'm now at...at the end of the road!" My mind went blank; I lost hope of him ever remembering what he had said to me that day on the train.

"Could you at least try to think before you open your mouth? You're at the end of the road, what does that have to do with me?! Unbelievable. Am I the one making you move? Why don't you go looking for that crazy fucking sister of yours?"

"Fine. Well, sir, I won't keep you from your meeting." His loathsome little speech had angered me so much I involuntarily slipped into formal address, my words spilling out haphazardly, unrestrained. "Fine, go ahead and return to your business. Goodbye. And after today, I guess we'll say that your life is your life, and mine is mine, just as if..."

"Excuse me? What did you say? Say that again to my face!" Jiang Songping's expression turned vicious and contorted; the condescension hissing between his teeth frightened me. "So now you're threatening me? Who are you? Who the fuck do you think you are? You want to end this friendship, is that it? You think I care? What did I ever do to you? How many clients have I sent your way? Every fucking red cent you ever made I earned for you, you know that? Don't forget that I even gave you that fucking shirt you're wearing right now! And you don't even give a shit! Fucking hell!"

The shouting and profanity must have disturbed the executives inside the conference room, for a couple of assistants scurried out and proceeded to drag him back in before he could finish. They urged him not to "bring yourself down to his level" and shot me looks of disgust before shutting the door.

Back home, I collapsed into bed with my clothes on, as if I had been hit with the flu. Images of Jiang Songping flooded over me when I closed my eyes. I saw him as a child, holding up those patched cotton trousers of his with one hand as he rolled that iron hoop through the shade down Mahogany Street, round and round again, the hoop heading silently toward me. They say the devil lives in our impulses; you can imagine how, as I lay there, filled with regret, I hated myself for my own recklessness. The world suddenly felt vast and hopeless. I knew that things were beyond fixing between us. And yet, for so many years, he had been the only friend I really cared about.

I drifted off to the rhythmic hammering of a pile driver at the construction site next door, falling into a murky sleep. One voice in my head questioned if I should rip off the Tommy Hilfiger shirt I was wearing and burn it. Another louder, more insistent, voice questioned if I should drive over to Songping's house, apologize, and ask for his forgiveness.

By the time the ringing of my cell phone woke me up, it was already past ten at night.

"Mr. Cui, I just wanted to tell you not to worry about sending me that recording. I found Leonhardt's albums online and downloaded them. I'm listening to one now," she said. "Can you hear it?"

Only after a long pause did I realize through the fuzziness of my brain that the call came from Sleeping Dragon Valley. The faint twanging of Leonhardt's harpsichord sounded unreal, as if echoing from a far-off world. I listened for a few more seconds, then mumbled that if she had no other business, I was going to hang up.

"What are you up to?" she asked.

"Nothing." I couldn't bother to be civil. I caught sight of a shirt I had hung on the radiator to dry—also a gift from Jiang Songping. My chest tightened up.

"Oh, what I wanted to ask is if you can see the night sky from where you are."

"What are you talking about?" I clambered out of bed, still holding my cell phone, and padded out onto the balcony.

"Can you see it?" she asked.

"See what?"

"Look up at the sky."

The rain had ceased long ago, and the northwest wind, which had been raging through the day, had also calmed. To the southwest, over the tops of the naked trees, you could see thick fingers of altocumulus, like cotton candy, or cauliflower. The deep, singular blue of the night sky brought the clouds into delicate relief, the scene evoking an air of mystery. I noticed among the brightest stars a glittering bowl with a handle—the legendary Big Dipper.

So did she want me to look at the clouds or the Dipper? I couldn't be sure, and didn't care enough to ask. Her ill-timed romantic insinuations irritated me immensely.

"Isn't it lovely?" she asked me. Unable to think of an inspired response, I played along and said, "Yes, it's beautiful," then lit a cigarette.

She asked me again about my living situation.

She said if I could find a nice apartment in the next few days that would be great, but if I couldn't, and needed to be out of my place before the year ended, I was welcome to stay with her for a while. I could tell she wasn't joking this time. She said she hadn't had a full night's sleep since Ding Caichen died. She had covered all the mirrors in the house. She started to suffer from hallucinations due to long-term sleep deprivation—whenever she looked in a mirror, she saw the fleeing shadow of Ding Caichen. Then the light would change, and the figure would be gone. Yet parts of him lingered behind, like a pair of underwear, or his old loafers. It felt like he had neither died nor left the house; she simply couldn't see him.

She went on to tell me that most of the residents in their neighborhood only stayed there on the weekends. The houses next to hers remained totally empty during the week; in the evenings the whole valley grew as dark and hollow as a tomb—it felt very eerie.

I could hear a touch of fear in her voice.

Finally she said, "If you really can't stand my face I can cover it."

After she hung up, I gazed out at that rare, pristine Beijing sky for a long while. For some reason, I felt a stinging sensation in my nose, and couldn't help but weep.

11. THE 300B

THE FOLLOWING afternoon, I called a moving company.

On December 31st, in the early hours of the morning, I moved to Sleeping Dragon Valley.

That evening, I drove back to Shijingshan and dropped the apartment key into my sister's hand. She didn't ask where I was going; she just cried and tried to hug me.

I backed away.

In October of the following year, I became the father of a beautiful baby daughter. Her mother and I never married. I didn't even know her mother's real name. She told me I could call her whatever I wanted. I tried calling her Yufen, which she actually answered to quite happily.

I once asked her if Ding Caichen had been part of the mafia. She replied equivocally, saying that whether he was or wasn't didn't matter; what mattered was that he was dead. Forget about him.

"But how could a mafioso be forced to commit suicide?" I continued.

"It only goes to show," she said, "that there are forces in this society more terrifying than the mafia. Ding Caichen was no match for them."

As to what those "terrifying forces" might be, I couldn't begin to imagine.

One day I pestered her to tell me her story. Where did she come from? How did she end up in a place like Sleeping Dragon Valley? Her accent sounded southern. She became evasive, avoided my gaze. Finally she sighed and gave me an elusive reply: "There's really nothing to tell—I was just one of Ding Caichen's hostages."

"You mean you were kidnapped?" I asked in shock.

"So were you, weren't you?" she mockingly replied.

I didn't know what the hell she meant. She seemed to be suggesting that I had been kidnapped and held hostage myself, but how could that be? Nothing had been wrong with me; I did what I needed to do, as a free man.

Now, when we do it together (what you'd rather call "making love"), I no longer need to hide her face with a pillowcase. Yet I still know next to nothing about her. Any information relating to her and her background has been strictly censored, just as her natural beauty has been censored by her mutilated face.

On one occasion, I stealthily searched the entire house, looking for photographs of her. I really wanted to see what she looked like before her injuries. My efforts were in vain.

"Oh, don't worry about it," she comforted me. "The day our daughter grows into a woman, there I'll be. How she'll look is exactly how I used to look."

Sometimes I'd talk to her about my mother. I'm not sure why, but the two times I brought up my mother's prediction, it seemed to depress her, and she grew quiet. I thought the subject annoyed her. That couldn't be it, though, because this past November, as our daughter approached her first month, she asked me if we could take the baby to my mother's grave. She wanted to pay her respects to the old woman.

That put me in a quandary, actually. Not because I didn't want to take her. As you know, after my mother died, my sister Cui Lihua took care of all the arrangements. I didn't know where my mother had been buried. Naturally, I'd never admit that to my wife. Nor could I think of any way to find out other than calling my sister to ask. I couldn't sleep at all that night. As dawn broke, I tiptoed downstairs and shut myself in the closet by the kitchen to phone my sister.

When my sister heard my voice, she didn't say anything but just started to sob. On and on she bawled, until she could finally stop, whereupon she began to whine for me to come home immediately. I asked her about Ma's grave but she paid me no heed. She only repeated her demand, over and over, that I come home as soon as possible so she could cook me fennel dumplings. As if all she owed me in this lifetime could be boiled down to a plate of fennel dumplings. I could feel myself about to cry. Only after my sister made me swear on my life to come home within the week did she tell me that Ma was buried next to our father at the Gold Summit Garden on Jade Spring Hill, not far from the Sleeping Buddha Temple. Take the 375 bus to Red Flag Village, walk through the cemetery gate, take the left-hand pathway to the top of the hill, then turn around and go back down—to the seventh row of headstones, sixth one across. She had planted a ginkgo tree in front of the grave earlier this year.

Two days later, the weather clear and calm, we took the baby to the cemetery. My wife wore a scarf wrapped tightly around her head. She told me this was the first time she had left Sleeping Dragon Valley since coming to Beijing. We stopped at a flower shop by the Summer Palace where she bought my mother a large bouquet of white calla lilies. She carefully placed the flowers in the back seat of the car, and as she took the baby from me, she remembered something. Touching my arm, she softly said, "Shouldn't we get something for Papa as well?" I liked the easy, affectionate way she said "Papa." She got out of the car again, ran into a shop, and returned with two bottles of Cowshed Mountain white liquor for my father.

Our daughter thought everything at the cemetery utterly fantastic. She climbed the hill in a carrier strapped against her mother's breast, kicking her little legs and exclaiming "Oh—oh—oh!" The late autumn scene preserved an exaggerated stillness; the sky above the treetops so blue it caused dizziness. After we paid our respects, with no one else around, we didn't bother to cut the stems off the lilies one by one. Observing the slender, ink-black ginkgo tree, I felt a twinge of regret—maybe I should've been a bit more open and agreed to take my sister with us.

My wife, clearly in a good mood as we ambled back down the hill, suggested that we find a place to have lunch and then go for a stroll around the botanical garden next to the Sleeping Buddha Temple. I readily agreed. But upon exiting the public toilet at the gate of the cemetery, I changed my mind. I told her that I had an upset stomach, and that we should head straight home.

I knew the look on my face must have been frightening.

I tried my hardest to control my anxiety and calm down a little, but the effort just made my anxiety worse. We got in the car and I drove like one possessed, settling into the fast lane and leaning on my horn the whole way home.

The whole ride I waited for her to ask me what was wrong. Had she done so, I would have told her everything about the text message I had received in the bathroom. But she just kept playing with the baby, seemingly oblivious to my changed mood. In that respect, she had a lot in common with Yufen.

Two hours later, I parked the car at the edge of the lot at the Sleeping Dragon Valley community center. The China Construction Bank ATM in the parking lot informed me that Ding Caichen's remaining two hundred and sixty thousand yuan had been paid in full to my account.

The story of Ding Caichen's death always seemed suspicious to me. I had tried several times before to coax my wife into revealing anything. But after that message dinged in from the bank, I was a little scared to bring it up.

"If you want my opinion, I think it's a good thing," my wife said one evening, as she patted the baby to sleep. "That two hundred and sixty thousand is yours by contract. You didn't steal or extort it, so we have no reason to be afraid. As to whether or not the man's really dead, you don't need to worry about it."

She was right, of course, but for the next three months I couldn't shake the image of Ding Caichen, coffee cup in hand, jumping off the top of a skyscraper in Dongzhimen. I couldn't bring myself to spend a single yuan of the money.

Every so often I'd complain to her that we couldn't live with this confusion for the rest of our lives. Although things were really great between us, I still felt lost, as if everything in my life were ambiguous. Could we really continue in this way?

My wife invariably responded with a smile and ended with another question. "You should understand that nothing in this world is ever truly clear. If life is crazy, let it be crazy! If you tried to live every single detail of your life with perfect clarity, you surely wouldn't even make it through the first day. Try to be perfect, and where's the fun?"

I carried on with my amplifier business.

My client in the Brownstones apparently had enough of his KT88. He asked me if I could build him a 300B instead, preferably with specialty-molded Level 3 Western Electric tubes, if I could find them. I tried to persuade him that the 300B really didn't match his Acapella speakers, but this angered the good professor, who ordered me to "Just shut up and do it."

Which I was all too willing to do, of course.

The day I brought the machine over, the professor sat, once again, at his kitchen table, this time lecturing his wife the volleyball coach on the awful condition of society. You know: corrupt social morality, destruction of irreplaceable traditions, the spiritual backbone of community broken by egotism and greed, and the rest of that bullshit. He concluded with the nugget of wisdom that no Chinese in today's society could possibly live a truly satisfying life. His wife, obviously tired of listening to him, sat hunched over at the table with her eyes lowered, unresponsive, texting furiously. Embarrassed at being ignored in such a way, the professor fell back on that old rhetorical figure which he still and used which I hated so damn much: "Am I right?"

I looked up at him from my work, and set down my screwdriver. Then I stood up, hitched up my pants, and said in a tone that surprised even me, "Do you mind if I contribute my thoughts to this one? If you could just stop nitpicking and dissecting every little thing, if you could learn to keep one eye closed and one eye open, and quit worrying about everything and everybody, you might discover that life is actually pretty fucking beautiful. Am I right?"

TITLES IN SERIES

For a complete list of titles, visit www.nyrb.com or write to:
Catalog Requests, NYRB, 435 Hudson Street, New York, NY 10014

J.R. ACKERLEY Hindoo Holiday*
J.R. ACKERLEY My Dog Tulip*
J.R. ACKERLEY My Father and Myself*
J.R. ACKERLEY We Think the World of You*
HENRY ADAMS The Jeffersonian Transformation
RENATA ADLER Pitch Dark*
RENATA ADLER Speedboat*
AESCHYLUS Prometheus Bound; translated by Joel Agee*
LEOPOLDO ALAS His Only Son *with* Doña Berta*
CÉLESTE ALBARET Monsieur Proust
DANTE ALIGHIERI The Inferno
DANTE ALIGHIERI The New Life
KINGSLEY AMIS The Alteration*
KINGSLEY AMIS Dear Illusion: Collected Stories*
KINGSLEY AMIS Ending Up*
KINGSLEY AMIS Girl, 20*
KINGSLEY AMIS The Green Man*
KINGSLEY AMIS Lucky Jim*
KINGSLEY AMIS The Old Devils*
KINGSLEY AMIS One Fat Englishman*
KINGSLEY AMIS Take a Girl Like You*
ROBERTO ARLT The Seven Madmen*
WILLIAM ATTAWAY Blood on the Forge
W.H. AUDEN (EDITOR) The Living Thoughts of Kierkegaard
W.H. AUDEN W.H. Auden's Book of Light Verse
ERICH AUERBACH Dante: Poet of the Secular World
DOROTHY BAKER Cassandra at the Wedding*
DOROTHY BAKER Young Man with a Horn*
J.A. BAKER The Peregrine
S. JOSEPHINE BAKER Fighting for Life*
HONORÉ DE BALZAC The Human Comedy: Selected Stories*
HONORÉ DE BALZAC The Unknown Masterpiece *and* Gambara*
VICKI BAUM Grand Hotel*
SYBILLE BEDFORD A Legacy*
SYBILLE BEDFORD A Visit to Don Otavio: A Mexican Journey*
MAX BEERBOHM The Prince of Minor Writers: The Selected Essays of Max Beerbohm*
MAX BEERBOHM Seven Men
STEPHEN BENATAR Wish Her Safe at Home*
FRANS G. BENGTSSON The Long Ships*
ALEXANDER BERKMAN Prison Memoirs of an Anarchist
GEORGES BERNANOS Mouchette
MIRON BIAŁOSZEWSKI A Memoir of the Warsaw Uprising*
ADOLFO BIOY CASARES Asleep in the Sun
ADOLFO BIOY CASARES The Invention of Morel
EVE BABITZ Eve's Hollywood*
EVE BABITZ Slow Days, Fast Company: The World, the Flesh, and L.A.*
CAROLINE BLACKWOOD Corrigan*

* *Also available as an electronic book.*

CAROLINE BLACKWOOD Great Granny Webster*
RONALD BLYTHE Akenfield: Portrait of an English Village*
NICOLAS BOUVIER The Way of the World
EMMANUEL BOVE Henri Duchemin and His Shadows*
MALCOLM BRALY On the Yard*
MILLEN BRAND The Outward Room*
SIR THOMAS BROWNE Religio Medici and Urne-Buriall*
JOHN HORNE BURNS The Gallery
ROBERT BURTON The Anatomy of Melancholy
CAMARA LAYE The Radiance of the King
GIROLAMO CARDANO The Book of My Life
DON CARPENTER Hard Rain Falling*
J.L. CARR A Month in the Country*
BLAISE CENDRARS Moravagine
EILEEN CHANG Love in a Fallen City
EILEEN CHANG Naked Earth*
JOAN CHASE During the Reign of the Queen of Persia*
ELLIOTT CHAZE Black Wings Has My Angel*
UPAMANYU CHATTERJEE English, August: An Indian Story
NIRAD C. CHAUDHURI The Autobiography of an Unknown Indian
ANTON CHEKHOV Peasants and Other Stories
ANTON CHEKHOV The Prank: The Best of Young Chekhov*
GABRIEL CHEVALLIER Fear: A Novel of World War I*
JEAN-PAUL CLÉBERT Paris Vagabond*
RICHARD COBB Paris and Elsewhere
COLETTE The Pure and the Impure
JOHN COLLIER Fancies and Goodnights
CARLO COLLODI The Adventures of Pinocchio*
D.G. COMPTON The Continuous Katherine Mortenhoe
IVY COMPTON-BURNETT A House and Its Head
IVY COMPTON-BURNETT Manservant and Maidservant
BARBARA COMYNS The Vet's Daughter
BARBARA COMYNS Our Spoons Came from Woolworths*
ALBERT COSSERY The Jokers*
ALBERT COSSERY Proud Beggars*
HAROLD CRUSE The Crisis of the Negro Intellectual
ASTOLPHE DE CUSTINE Letters from Russia*
LORENZO DA PONTE Memoirs
ELIZABETH DAVID A Book of Mediterranean Food
ELIZABETH DAVID Summer Cooking
L.J. DAVIS A Meaningful Life*
AGNES DE MILLE Dance to the Piper*
VIVANT DENON No Tomorrow/Point de lendemain
MARIA DERMOÛT The Ten Thousand Things
DER NISTER The Family Mashber
TIBOR DÉRY Niki: The Story of a Dog
ANTONIO DI BENEDETTO Zama
JEAN D'ORMESSON The Glory of the Empire: A Novel, A History*
ARTHUR CONAN DOYLE The Exploits and Adventures of Brigadier Gerard
CHARLES DUFF A Handbook on Hanging
BRUCE DUFFY The World As I Found It*
DAPHNE DU MAURIER Don't Look Now: Stories
ELAINE DUNDY The Dud Avocado*
ELAINE DUNDY The Old Man and Me*

G.B. EDWARDS The Book of Ebenezer Le Page*

JOHN EHLE The Land Breakers*

MARCELLUS EMANTS A Posthumous Confession

EURIPIDES Grief Lessons: Four Plays; translated by Anne Carson

J.G. FARRELL Troubles*

J.G. FARRELL The Siege of Krishnapur*

J.G. FARRELL The Singapore Grip*

ELIZA FAY Original Letters from India

KENNETH FEARING The Big Clock

KENNETH FEARING Clark Gifford's Body

FÉLIX FÉNÉON Novels in Three Lines*

M.I. FINLEY The World of Odysseus

THOMAS FLANAGAN The Year of the French*

BENJAMIN FONDANE Existential Monday: Philosophical Essays*

SANFORD FRIEDMAN Conversations with Beethoven*

SANFORD FRIEDMAN Totempole*

MASANOBU FUKUOKA The One-Straw Revolution*

MARC FUMAROLI When the World Spoke French

CARLO EMILIO GADDA That Awful Mess on the Via Merulana

BENITO PÉREZ GÁLDOS Tristana*

MAVIS GALLANT The Cost of Living: Early and Uncollected Stories*

MAVIS GALLANT Paris Stories*

MAVIS GALLANT A Fairly Good Time *with* Green Water, Green Sky*

MAVIS GALLANT Varieties of Exile*

GABRIEL GARCÍA MÁRQUEZ Clandestine in Chile: The Adventures of Miguel Littín

LEONARD GARDNER Fat City*

ALAN GARNER Red Shift*

WILLIAM H. GASS In the Heart of the Heart of the Country: And Other Stories*

WILLIAM H. GASS On Being Blue: A Philosophical Inquiry*

THÉOPHILE GAUTIER My Fantoms

GE FEI The Invisibility Cloak

JEAN GENET Prisoner of Love

ÉLISABETH GILLE The Mirador: Dreamed Memories of Irène Némirovsky by Her Daughter*

JEAN GIONO Hill*

JOHN GLASSCO Memoirs of Montparnasse*

P.V. GLOB The Bog People: Iron-Age Man Preserved

NIKOLAI GOGOL Dead Souls*

EDMOND AND JULES DE GONCOURT Pages from the Goncourt Journals

PAUL GOODMAN Growing Up Absurd: Problems of Youth in the Organized Society*

EDWARD GOREY (EDITOR) The Haunted Looking Glass

JEREMIAS GOTTHELF The Black Spider*

A.C. GRAHAM Poems of the Late T'ang

WILLIAM LINDSAY GRESHAM Nightmare Alley*

HANS HERBERT GRIMM Schlump*

EMMETT GROGAN Ringolevio: A Life Played for Keeps

VASILY GROSSMAN An Armenian Sketchbook*

VASILY GROSSMAN Everything Flows*

VASILY GROSSMAN Life and Fate*

VASILY GROSSMAN The Road*

OAKLEY HALL Warlock

PATRICK HAMILTON The Slaves of Solitude*

PATRICK HAMILTON Twenty Thousand Streets Under the Sky*

PETER HANDKE Short Letter, Long Farewell

PETER HANDKE Slow Homecoming